MW00761941

CHRISTOPHER'S ADVENTURES

IN

EVERGREEN

CHRISTOPHER'S ADVENTURES

IN

EVERGREEN

by

Wendy Cincotta

Illustrations by Eva Cincotta

Edited by Nan Fornal

Evergreen Books

To Jonathan

TABLE OF CONTENTS

CHRISTOPHER'S ADVENTURES

IN

EVERGREEN

~ CHAPTER I ~

THE TALL SIR

This is the story of Christopher, and how he met a tree named Sir TwoThreeFourFiveSixSeven-Two.

On that cool and blustery August day, Christopher did not think that he had wandered far off. It was chilly . . . too chilly for late summer, too chilly to be having a family picnic. It was midday, and he was bored.

Christopher had found it more interesting to sit with the adults and listen to their conversation than to play with his cousins, until a serious topic came up and someone said, "Christopher, why don't you go play with your cousins?"

His cousins had been running around as usual, wrestling, playing rough, and teasing the girls. A few of the younger adults were getting ready to organize a three-legged race. Meanwhile, Grandpa Jon had dozed off by the barbecue just next to where Uncle Hal was broiling steaks. Uncle Hal was being particularly annoying, loudly telling the same old jokes at the grill while he turned the steaks. Christopher had grown less and less fond of him recently. He seemed to be at their house all the time, and Christopher's father had died just six months ago. This seemed as good a time as any to wander off on his own.

Besides, that was when he noticed the bird.

It was the kind of bird one would expect to see at the pet store or in a book about distant places: a bright bird with a light blue stripe on the tail. It was not a cardinal, but had a distinctly fiery orange hue. It was small and flitted fast over a treetop just as Christopher was pondering the right moment to make his escape. It flitted over another tree, then swept down and through as it entered the forest.

Christopher had often been called too curious for his own good, and sometimes brave—though it was really his overriding curiosity, and not bravery, that caused him to investigate things. Indeed, he often did feel afraid at certain times. His heart would race and his face would flush, but if he was curious enough, his feet seemed to take him onward, or words seemed to come out of his mouth on their own. At first he had gone only as far as the edge of the field—to the towering wall of forest. Gone were the shouts and sounds of the family games behind him. They had faded like the sun in the afternoon sky, which ducked behind clouds the closer he had come to the trees. Christopher tightened his jacket against the breeze that came from the edge of the field and parted his brown hair. He smelled the scents of pine and earth as the cool from the quiet, dense shade wafted toward him.

He could not remember when he had entered the cool shade and begun to tread upon dry dirt and leaves, leaving the soft brushes of grass behind. He wandered for much of the afternoon, lost in his own thoughts and play. Now he stood stationary in the forest. There was less sun, more silence. He paused to realize how much silence there was about him, and how long it had been since he had seen the field nearby. The only noise had been that of his own thoughts, and now his thoughts were quieted as he wondered from which direction he had come.

Everything looked the same no matter which way Christopher turned. The field had been behind him, to his left . . . or was it right? Such a strange thing, that he could not remember how many circles he had made in this spot as he examined the party of trees about him. Had he turned around often? Had it been a half turn or a full turn? Did he turn twice? If he turned twice, was the field still to the left? From which direction had he come?

Christopher became dizzy just standing there, thinking and looking up, turning around and pondering the direction of his feet. Without coming to any conclusion, he began again to walk.

The sun was gone from the sky, hidden in clouds, bringing a cool that was more sobering, making him realize that the end of the day was approaching. Christopher looked down at his feet, which moved steadily along. His shoes were covered with the dust of a forest dirt. He tightened his red jacket around him and let a yawn have its full way as his mouth stretched to a size that surprised him. His eyes teared over, making the sticks in his path more visible. He blinked his eyes, and they filled up again. A feeling of worry settled in upon him. His head and legs felt the wear of what must have been hours of walking.

He stopped. Taking a deep breath, he looked about with a renewed sense of energy. Soon, it would be dark, and the thought of spending a cold night in the woods was not a comforting one. *Perhaps if I think . . . not of where my feet* came from *but to where they should go, then I shall find my way back,* thought Christopher. So he searched the ground for just the right spot upon which to stand. But, then, it really didn't matter, for everything looked the same.

Didn't it?

He stopped.

For there, on the ground, something had caught his eye.

He thought for a moment as the image lingered before him. He had seen. . . . Had he seen? No. Yes. There, on the ground, in the flatness of dirt . . . it looked like . . . ! Was it? What a curious thing. And looking back, he saw that he had been correct: It looked like an arrow.

There before him lay three sticks, not one on top of another but all lying flat and touching perfectly. Two were smaller and equal to each other. The third was longer. Together, they were unmistakably . . . yes, an arrow, about eight inches long.

Christopher crouched, his face close to the ground, examining this phenomenon. Unfortunate, too, that there was no one here to whom he could show the arrow (although perhaps he would have been accused by Tom Shanksbury of making it himself while no one else watched, and that it was all a gag to embarrass whoever was silly enough to believe him). But there was no one about. At least, he thought there had been no one. Certainly, he had neither heard nor seen any moving thing.

As he crouched there, another thought occurred that caused the hairs on Christopher's forearms to stand up momentarily; he felt slightly paralyzed for a second, for the arrow pointed to his left, and he had not, since discovering it, peered in that direction. So taken was he by the arrow that he had not thought to look to where it pointed.

Silence. All was quiet around him. He heard not the chirp of a bird nor the scurry of an animal. He remained there, staring beyond the arrow, afraid to look to the left. For now he felt that perhaps there was something there. Yes, surely. Just then, the sun came through the clouds, casting a bit of warmth and glare down through the trees, on the ground and upon his coat, upon his left side, shining before it would disappear completely for the night. Now, with the warm rays pouring down on him and trickling through the leaves, Christopher decided to turn his head slowly. He would look before darkness came. He would turn his head to the left as slowly as the sun had come into view out of the clouds, so as not to be noticed. To the left and toward a shadow that was on the ground . . . when a sound came to Christopher's ears that sent him falling over, dizzy and shaken and upside down.

"WELL, HELL-LOOOWE!!! HELL-LOOOWE . . . HELL-LOOOWE . . . HELL-LOOOWE!" This deep sound seemed to vibrate the very ground upon which Christopher lay—he, looking up and trying to see—but the glare of the sun blocked his view of something tall, as tall as the sun, towering up to where the sun was. He lay there, astonished, blinking, squinting, heart pounding in his chest, unable to move or do anything but squint up and above, trying to see what he could not.

"WELL, I DIDN'T MEAN TO FRIGHTEN YOU, LAD!" came the voice again, like an echo and full of mirth, vibrating Christopher's bones like the drums in a parade. Christopher's only movement came from his hand, which emerged to block the sun.

"FOR HEAVEN'S SHOES, LAD, I HOPE YOU'RE ALL RIGHT LYING THERE. I SAY, CAN YOU HEAR ME, LAD?"

And then the sun began to pass. As slowly as it had come, it began to pass behind a cloud, steadily, until Christopher could finally see the shape before him. He could see the form of a man, dressed like . . . a soldier . . . so very tall—perhaps eleven feet! And very thin, like a post, with long arms that were stretched out in expression, not down at his sides. Christopher could not help but think that this man looked very much like a tree.

"Here, lad, let me help you," came the voice, still loud but not nearly so booming as before. Although the voice's owner now seemed more human, Christopher gave a start as he approached, for his arms were strange under his uniform, his face smooth as if shaven by a tool, his cap so high it might be concealing a point, legs that moved stiffly without much giving, and a middle that seemed hollow of anything that would allow digestion or the flow of blood.

"Here, man," he said, "Let's get you standing now. It's not good to see you lying there. Nothing to be frightened about now. It's only me, just Bruce here, Bruce the Spruce. If you wouldn't mind terribly, I'll ask you not to call me that," he said as he helped Christopher to his feet, slipping branchlike arms under Christopher's elbows, sending a chill through Christopher that caused his vision to sway. Christopher sensed both strength and frailty in the branches: The strength came forth from somewhere, possibly the trunk, but the arms or, rather, branches, were slightly thin. It was not surprising that they grew thinner toward the edges.

Indeed!

Christopher, standing now only a few feet away from this resonating voice before him, looked upon the shiny buttons on the worn uniform. He let his eyes travel up, way up the form to the shaven and slightly handsome face, to eyes that were alive and as real as his own, a long thin nose of wood, lips large and red and expressive. He looked down at Christopher, the little mole upon his chin resembling a tiny knot. For this man was not a man. This man was a tree.

Well, lad, you're up! Glad to see you so and sorry that you had a fall! I've had a few of them, too, you know. Really takes a toll on the leaves, eh?" And he laughed heartily and stiffly, squinting when he did so. He seemed unable to move to the extent that his expressions wished. "Well, what's wrong, son? For heaven's shoes, can't you talk at all? And if you can, I'll have you know my true andonly name. It is what I am called and prefer to be called . . . provided you CAN speak."

When Christopher opened his mouth to speak, something failed in his throat, and the words did not come. Clearing his throat, blushing, and taking a step back, he rested his neck, which had been straining as he stared up and above. Looking around he turned back to the tree and tried again to speak. "What . . ." he said, the word coming out in a whisper. He opened his mouth, and, feeling his face grow hot, could only murmur, " . . . is it?"

The tree responded immediately, happy to be asked. He stepped back as if he were a general overlooking a front, and then he turned stiffly to face Christopher. Closing his eyes, with one branch stretched behind and the other royally outstretched, he proudly announced:

"I am Sir TwoThreeFourFiveSixSeven-Two. And you, young lad, may call me such." This formality ended, the tree relaxed into friendliness, and asked, "Well?"

Christopher looked up at the tree.

The tree paused and then asked, "Do you have a name?"

"Christopher," he replied.

"A fine name," the tree said. "Well, don't be so surprised to see me, lad, I'm just your friendly neighborhood tree. Neighborhood, but not happy about it. Fact is, I really belong on the war front, if you know what I mean. This civilian stuff is just not for me. Hearty hemlocks what's wrong son?"

"But, you can't be."

"But I am," answered the tree.

Christopher circled the tree, who stood up proudly, if not vainly. "You are?"

"I am."

"But how?"

"How's that?"

"How can you be, er, walking?"

"I've woken up, of course."

"Trees don't wake up. Maybe I've been walking too long – I'm seeing things."

"Well, they do in Evergreen."

"Evergreen? Is that where you're from?"

"Quite so. Anyway, you should probably head that way," the tree pointed with a branch which ended in several crooked fingers.

"So you put the arrow there?"

"Yes. Sacrificed a few fingers for that."

The tree stiffly reached into the pocket of his uniform and retrieved a brown pouch fastened with a cord. Christopher watched the coordinated, small branches on the limbs' ends, the joints which imitated elbow and shoulder.

"If you don't mind my prying, Christopher," the tree continued, "it would appear that you are on a mission and have gone off your coordinates. Therefore, I would not be hard-pressed to escort you on your direct way back to . . . to . . . to wherever it is you happen to be heading."

"Do you know the way back to the field?" Christopher interrupted anxiously. For just then the air around them had become a shade darker. The tree looked back at him in surprise, and had it not gotten still darker, Christopher would have sworn he had seen the tree grow slightly pale.

The tree, now reaching into his pocket and pulling out a pouch, answered, "I'm sorry to say, friend, that I do not understand your word 'field' nor what it means. I suppose that it is where you are from . . . 'Field.' " The tree stopped, lifting his head slightly, the dark shape staring off quietly. "I'm not sure what it is about that place, but I do say that something gives me a strange feeling when I hear of it—something that I might not like. . . . Oh, I am sorry, friend, I didn't mean to offend you."

Maybe because there are no trees there, thought Christopher. With that, the tree rubbed a blue paste on the end of a stick. The tree closed the pouch and placed it back into his pocket. He reached into another pocket, brought something against his cheek and, after a scratching sound, there was a small flame and Christopher could once again see the tree's face. The tree smiled, looked up at the stick and said, "Stand back, lad, it sparks for a moment."

And with that, a torch was lit.

"Anyway, let's be off," continued the tree, "to the east and to the right, for I am not sure I can take you back to 'Field,' but I can try to bring you to its vicinity. For quaking aspens, that word gives me the downright shivers."

And with the torch burning like a spotlight above them they walked. Christopher walked warily, observing the tree's rootlike feet, his stiff walk, the burning arm. He followed the firelight's glow and soon came to the tree's side. The forest was now blackening around them. Christopher felt comforted by this presence . . . this someone . . . a friend, and did not consider for too long what the evening would have been like without him.

~ CHAPTER II ~

THE DARK WOOD

And so it was that they walked, in silence and through the cool night air. There was no breeze, no sound of stirring animals or birds, just the two figures moving with stealth in the vast darkness about them that went on for miles. They moved in the dim glowing bit of light held high by the tree, Christopher staying close beside and looking about. He was surprised to see just how dark it had become.

"Sir . . . " Christopher said, looking out into the quiet blackness. He felt slightly afraid and continued on in the lowest whisper he could muster, " . . . why is it . . . " And then he lowered his voice even more, for it was very silent, indeed, and he thought his voice had echoed a little: "Why is it that these other trees do not move?"

"There's no need to whisper, friend, we shall walk farther to the north now," the tree pointed. "They can't hear you, lad, they're all asleep. And might I say that I would rather burn my own limb than exist in a world of dark and density. Thank heaven's shoes I have been recruited to awaken."

"Sir . . . " he queried after a while, looking at the dulled, faded uniform, and curious to hear the tree speak, " . . . er, Sir TwoThreeFourFiveSixSeven-Two, how did you become a soldier?"

"Well," the tree replied, beginning as he nearly always did with pleasant interest, "I suppose I have always been a soldier but hadn't always known it, and always will be one now and in the future whether I am told that I am or that I am not. Whether I am active or inactive in duty and service, you see I am still forever a soldier. Sometimes not aware of it, sometimes not it fully, sometimes told by others that they think that of me not. Sometimes not realizing it my very self, mind you, but certainly a soldier in thought and manner and in being and action. Does that answer it?" the tree said.

"But who told you that you were not?"

The tree continued. "Well, they did, lad, of course," he had a look of slight astonishment, "for they may call me that common name of Spruce who existed before I was thankfully awakened, but it matters not for I know that I am a Sir, in my core and layers of bark I am, and this they cannot take away, no matter what is done."

"But who, Sir TwoThreeFourFiveSixSeven-Two, who are they?"

At this the tree acted startled again. He was quiet, looked speechless and astonished, and did not answer Christopher but merely searched the forest in surprise. They walked farther on through the trees into what seemed an even denser wood. The tree's torch burned steadily, lighting their way, illuminating the night around them.

"There is a war about to rage in Evergreen," the tree answered finally, "and many of my kind are not prepared fight. They have been lulled into ignoring that some of our trees have become dangerously driven by greed."

"Where is Evergreen?"

The tree pointed. "That way."

"Are there a lot of trees that are awake there?"

"Yes."

"How come I've never seen any?"

"Well, you have to have a key, of course."

"A key."

"To get into Evergreen. Through the Air Door."

"What's an Air Door?"

"My goodness, but you are uninformed? It is a door between two trees."

"Really?! How did you happen to come through the door?"

"I came through to help you. This is a night when the boundaries between your world and ours are blurred. We may see other trees, or shadows of other trees, for a very brief time."

"Is it a holiday?"

"Not exactly. It's a way that the doors are renewed, freed from debris that may have become caught in them over the years. Happens only once every seven years."

They had walked for three quarters of an hour. Christopher was deep in thought over the tree's words. Occasionally, he looked up at the tree. Then he yawned.

"You know, lad, it occurs to me that you by this time may be needing some nourishment of a kind, you being so fleshy and all. I know where we might head if you think you need something to carry you over on our way back. Considering the length you have behind you, and the length before us, well, you're looking rather pale, lad."

Christopher was feeling pale. He hadn't eaten much at the picnic and had been in the forest all day. He was suddenly very hungry at the mention of food. But he was more curious to know about the tree.

The tree changed direction, and they continued on for another quarter of an hour. And then, as he seemed to search more furtively about them, holding the torch high in the air, a voice emerged from the shadows, startling Christopher. It was melodic, high in pitch, and coming from their right.

"Two? Is that you, Two? How in heaven's feet are you, you old fir, you! Come here so I can have a look at you. It is you, isn't it?"

Christopher followed the Sir's movement of the torch.

"My good Madam," the tree replied, "if you would be so kind as to address me by my true and only name, I would be very much obliged."

The light revealed a shape, wide and low to the ground. There was movement; it was another tree, but this one a stump. The stump's eyes were wide and large, with eyelashes and features similar to the Sir's: a long wooden nose and large lips that moved freely and expressively. It was a she tree, and she wore no hat, nor a uniform.

"And," Sir Two continued, "might I remind you, Madam, that my breeding is of the Spruce type, and not of the Fir . . . "

"Oh, what's the difference, you old gump. You're still a tree! And so thin you've become since I saw you last," she continued. "And what's this you've brought me, a human squirrel? Hm?"

Christopher came forward and introduced himself, even though he felt terribly strange doing so. The Stump responded delightedly.

"As you see, Madam, he is not of the squirolus species," said Sir Two.

"Well, now, a real boy," she said, "and very pleased to know you. I am Neddy, of the Oaks, and fully awake at this time."

NEDDY THE STUMP

"Yes, Madam," Sir Two replied. "Now if it would not seem rude, we would apologize that we cannot stay for very long but would hope you might have something about if it is not inconvenient, for you see our visitor is in need of some victuals and we would be semipressed to continue our mission of a kind of . . . well . . . a return of sorts."

"Oh, fine, fine, glad to have you. What is it that you'd like?" she asked, and her branches began to move. Sir Two scrambled about, located a large stick, and placed it firmly into the ground. The pouch from his pocket emerged, and he set ablaze a new torch, then set off in a huff for kindling, mumbling something about the time.

Christopher tried to imagine what he would eat. With the vine-like arms the Stump gathered materials and in no time had miraculously prepared for them a meal.

They sat around the fire that Sir Two had built, Christopher on the ground and Sir Two in the most curious position, as if he himself had assumed the form of a chair, or as if sitting on a chair, but not really sitting upon anything at all. His knees were bent, round, and perfectly carved in their sockets. Christopher was not shy about studying this; he crouched on his hands and knees and looked underneath Sir Two to see the secret of this feat. Sir Two took no notice but talked on with the Stump, who was stationary in her position and serving things from all around. She served a type of meal similar to rice but with several kinds of nuts, spicy and served warm; a meat dish not unlike ham, salty and chewy, smoked and burnt at the edges; applesauce with cinnamon sprigs, steaming and hot; fruit juice that tasted like wine; and a hot, sweet berry dessert. Sir Two ate only the meat dish and the fruit wine. The Stump ate the rice dish and applesauce. And Christopher, well, he ate everything. He listened intently to their conversation once he had stopped his preoccupation with the invisible chair, but did not understand the things of which they spoke. They sat for a long time, the warm glow of the campfire and the voices eventually sending him into a deep sleep.

~ ~ ~

He awoke to the voices still conversing. For a moment Christopher did not know where he was. He could feel the dark cool of the forest in the air and through the ground beneath him, but he felt warmed by the hissing embers of the fire. The voices were steady and low, rising only from time to time.

"Well, I think it is a good thing, if you ask me, these changes were bound to happen sometime, and maybe I am not up on everything that is current, but I have ear knots to hear and know quite a bit. I'm not asleep, you know, and I certainly haven't given myself over to a number as you have, Sir Two."

"Precisely my point, Madam. It is not the number that is of issue here. The number is a mere means to mobility, to maintaining freedom so that one can eventually fight what will become the branding system, when they will not merely give us numbers but brand them upon our very bark," said Sir Two.

"But, Two, you've been branded just by taking the number to begin with, don't you see? It's not enough to just resist it when it becomes a burn on your bark. You've taken it, don't you see? You've left the forest."

"But, Madam," the Sir reasoned, "to serve my forest and as a mobile tree I must accept my order at the present time. And that order is for Sir TwoThreeFourFiveSixSeven-Two. I am thankful to be awakened, and so will serve my forest as best I can in thankfulness. If it comes to branding, then we shall withdraw. It is not the same for you, Madam, if you don't mind my saying so, for you have chosen immobility."

"How does a tree become awake?" asked Christopher suddenly, and at that the two trees turned to him, staring, wide-eyed and silent. They looked at each other without expression for some time.

Sir Two looked back to Christopher and said, "That's a big question, son."

"Why?" asked Christopher. "Who woke you up? Where were you before? And why is it that you walk and she doesn't?"

Sir Two answered slowly, "Well, I came from the Northeast section, that I know. And by my rings I was thirty-two seasons past, and . . . "

"I was seventy-eight," the Stump interrupted, "and not completely immobile," she said, turning to the Sir, "I'll have you know," her vinelike arms wriggling along the ground.

"Your arms can neither hear nor see, Madam, and so it matters not what distance they travel," answered Sir Two matter-of-factly.

"But how does a tree become awake?" Christopher persisted.

Again the trees looked blankly at Christopher and then at each other. Sir Two replied slowly, "Well . . . I . . . don't exactly know."

"You don't know?" Christopher was disappointed. "How could you not know?"

"Well, how did you come to think yourself, if you're so knowledgeable on the subject?"

"To think? I . . . well, I suppose I have always thought so long as I have been alive. I . . . I've got a brain. That's why!"

"Look, lad, we won't solve anything by making comparisons here since we are obviously two different species. How a tree becomes awake is one of the Mysteries of Evergreen."

"Mysteries? What are those?"

"Look, it is getting late and we have real travel still ahead of us, so if you are well stocked, then I'd say it's time to pack a lunch, just in case, and head west." the tree answered, rising to prepare to leave.

Christopher readied himself also, assuming he had broached a delicate topic. He did not make matters any better with his next inquiry.

"How is it that you're so sure of direction?"

This time the Sir looked completely befuddled, as if this was the silliest question in the world to be posed to a tree, and the Stump gave a laugh of nervous surprise as she scuttled about putting things away and wrapping a parcel.

"Why, Christopher. Every single, life-giving moment by which I live and breathe, forever up to this moment and always will it be, I know because I know . . . not from myself but for, because . . . it is . . . the Wind . . . that always tells me so."

"Goodbye! Bye now! Don't forget to send a leaf in the wind from time to time! Keep your head low!"

Christopher did not understand this last statement, but he was growing accustomed to the unexplainable. Whoever Neddy was, he was glad to have known her. As they set out, he looked upon Sir Two thankfully. For where would he be without him this evening? He noticed that Sir Two's hand was beginning to burn down, and his arm, becoming shorter ever so gradually. Christopher was touched by this, and possibly homesick, so for a moment he allowed himself to shed a tear. He dared not let Sir Two see this as he looked the other way.

They had walked all of twenty minutes when, as Sir Two was explaining military stratagem, he stopped, exclaiming, "Good heavens, man!"

And with that had burst into a sprint that made Christopher, upon first instinct, want to laugh.

"Boy!" Sir Two yelled, running away and Christopher now running after him, still wanting to laugh at the stiff legs and erect head resisting the speed of his run.

He could hear Sir Two up ahead, shouting something, and realized that they were not running away from something but, rather, after something. Christopher tried to catch up, and, indeed, he did with much effort, but only fell behind again when he heard Sir Two cry out, "Jumping junipers!" He simply could not help himself. In the run the torch had flickered out. This sent Christopher running even faster in the dark.

"Sir Two! Wait!" He was glad that he had already tried out this abbreviation of Sir Two's name beforehand, for, certainly, the long version would not be practical now. Sir Two must have heard him, for he shouted something in reply, a kind of growl that Christopher could not decipher.

They ran at full speed for what must have been ten more minutes. At some point Christopher had lost the parcel the Stump had given him. Sir Two began to slow down, bent over a bit in his stance, and when Christopher came upon him, he had come to a complete stop.

"Sshhh!" Sir Two looked around them in a circle and fumbled for a match. "There!" He pointed to a tree. Christopher looked and saw movement. Something darted out to another tree, then darted out to another. When Sir Two lit the match, Christopher saw a tiny scurrying shape, almost human, run about them in a circle, and then with speed that neither of them could ever follow, with the sound and force of a rocket, it shot out into the woods again.

Sir Two stood still in amazement for a moment, his eyes darting around them, at Christopher, and at the trees. Still hunched over, he stood with the match, and then finally lit again his smoldering arm. Christopher was out of breath, trying to catch his wind and speak at the same time. Sir Two hardly showed signs of breathing. He just stood upright and smiled.

"Did you not see that, boy?!!" Sir Two exclaimed.

"What?" Christopher asked, "If I knew you liked . . . chasing . . . squirrels . . . I would have suggested . . . it be done in the . . . daytime . . . and not in the middle of the . . . night!"

"Squirrels?" said Sir Two incredulously. "Is that what you think? Well, of all the— Son, I will have you know that what we have witnessed is nothing of the trivial, nothing of the squirolus species, that you have just been witness to, nothing less than a shooting elf!"

"A shooting elf? What in the world is a shooting elf?"

"My boy, must I explain everything? Oh, I beg your pardon. I am forgetting that you are not from Evergreen. You have just been witness to not just any mere elf but the rarest of the kind: a shooting elf. Shooting elves are smaller than regular elves, and they travel almost constantly. No one really knows where they rest. But when they pass through the forest, I can tell you it is not very often and it is a sign of great luck, and if one can follow it, one should. My boy, don't you see?"

Christopher was not very impressed. He still did not completely believe. It could have been an animal, but it did look human, and no animal could travel like a rocket. . . .

"How do they run so fast?" he asked suspiciously.

"Ah," was the reply, "if we knew that, then we would know one of the Seven Mysteries now, wouldn't we? The residents of Evergreen have tried to solve that one for centuries. Good question, my boy, good question."

"Seven Mysteries? What are the Seven Mysteries?" Christopher was breathing normally now.

Sir Two paused, and then looked at him seriously. "I will tell you three, which are of the Seven: one you already know, and another you have already asked. The third is this: Where did the Air Doors come from?" Sir Two himself looked curious.

"Air Doors? What are they, Sir Two? And what are the other questions, the other two or, rather, six?"

"Mysteries boy, Mysteries. How does a tree become awake? You've asked that one yourself. And what gives the shooting elf its speed? Those are the two, and I have offered only three. As for the third, it is not what are they but where did the Air Doors come from, or, if you prefer, why are they? Yes, one could say rightly that why are they is a more appropriate translation. As for what they are, well, they're precisely that, they're self-explanatory, they are Doors in the Air."

"Can you really open a door in the air?" asked Christopher.

"Ah, but it's not just any door. It is a door between two trees, and not just any two trees. You have to know where the Air Doors are. And, you have to have a key and a watch."

"What's the watch for?"

"It must be opened when the second hand passes twelve. And, you must also know where the keyhole is. Very important."

"Wow."

"Take, for example, this door," the tree stopped, pointing at two trees that were relatively close. "Now. This is an Evergreen Air Door. Some doors go only to Evergreen, others go to other places."

"Other places?"

"Yes. Now. The coordinates for this keyhole are right about – here. And when that second hand hits the twelve, it will give a little tug. And then—"

"Would you show me?" Christopher said in wonderment.

Sir Two paused. "I would advise against that. We are almost to the East where I suppose Field is. Not many from there come here, you know, and it's best if you . . . another time, lad, another day."

"But, Sir, what time is it? If I go back now, I may never come back. And if they haven't missed me, I should have to wait until morning anyway."

"Not missed you? They must be looking for you now, boy! No, that won't do. Come now, we've almost made it back."

"But the elf, Sir Two! You said yourself that the shooting elf was good luck! And he led us to the North, or Southeast, or . . . won't you take me with you? Maybe I can help you in return for all you've done for—"

"Help me? With what? You're not trained in the procedures of war, lad, you haven't a natural sense of direction, you cannot run long distances without heaving, you're human and so need regular sustenance of foodstuffs, you're small and not possessing of any great muscular strength. Pardon me, but I cannot continue without embarrassing you to a greater extent. Now, you may follow me or remain here in the dark."

"Wait!" Christopher yelled as Sir Two began walking, jumping up upon a rock. "I've got something!"

Sir Two turned, shedding his light upon Christopher, who had climbed a rock, and squinted. "Boy, get down from there. And what are you shouting about?"

"I've got something, Sir Two, that perhaps no one in Evergreen has!"

"Is that so? And what's that, boy?"

"Come closer," Christopher yelled.

Sir Two walked over and, looking up, said, "Now, what is it?"

"With all respect Sir," Christopher said as he knocked with his knuckles upon Sir Two's head: "I've got a human brain, and if you will allow me, I'd like to use it . . . to find out how it is that a tree becomes awake."

~ CHAPTER III ~

AIR DOORS

For the first time Christopher thought he saw Sir Two lose his temper—for just a fleeting moment—for his eyes jiggled slightly, and his forehead became pink. "All right, Mr. Smart Pants. If you will do nothing but insist upon this, then have it you will. I will warn you of warfare that is going on, not yet full-fledged, but still upon us in Evergreen, and—oh, for heaven's shoes—would you stop jumping around like that as if it were Herring Day for the Polars? What? Well, of course, we have Polar bears."

Sir Two sighed a tired sigh. "Aren't you tired, son?"

"No," Christopher said. He really was not, for he had dozed by the fireside as Sir Two and the Stump had talked, and, besides, he was too excited now to sleep.

"I'll have you know that you'll only peer through them, and then we will be back again. If you protest, I shall be forced to abandon you. I speak for your own good, son. In the meantime, turn that jacket of yours inside out for the color is too conspicuous," said the tree.

At that, Sir Two began to walk around, mumbling, carefully examining the trees, until he came upon two trees markedly close to one another, as if they were a doorway. He reached into his pocket and pulled out the pocket watch and a  gold key. He checked the watch and said, "Come on then, lad." Christopher ran to him, peering between the trees before them. He looked at Sir Two's pocket watch. When the second hand was at the ten, Sir Two placed the key in the air between the trees, just about where a keyhole might be. As the second hand approached the twelve, Sir Two breathed in deeply. Christopher did the same, not knowing why but taking as much air in as he could and keeping his eyes on Sir Two. Three seconds, two . . .

Sir Two exhaled and blew out the torch with one long breath. Christopher did the same, seeing only the smoke from the torch and Sir Two's shape turning the key. Suddenly, the smoke swirled upward, then back fast, and Christopher's breath was lost in a gust of wind that overtook them with a force that blew his hair and jacket back. He strained to open his eyes in the howling breeze. A small, at first undetectable circle of light formed between the trees, growing until it filled the square space between them. It was . . .

Sunlight. There before them, between the trees. It was the other side of the forest, in perfect daylight through the door, glimmering through on the other side as they stood in the middle of night's darkness. From the moment that Sir Two had blown out the torch and turned the key, many things had begun to happen. Almost at once, Christopher could hear a thumping, a marching sound, the even stomp of feet and low voices that chanted along in the march. It sounded as though they were getting nearer. As Christopher was trying to open his eyes, Sir Two said, "Oh! It's eleven-thirty! Hurry, boy!" and Christopher felt the brush of a branch upon his sleeve. "Go through the trees and follow close behind me!" No sooner had they passed through the trees that the door of dark behind them disappeared, and Christopher stood stunned and squinting in the daylight. He felt a tug and turned to see a whole league of trees approaching them. They looked like Sir Two but younger and bulkier. This struck Christopher as curious since a tree grows larger with age, but it was due to their differing, lighter breed. They wore bright blue uniforms and white hats. They marched neatly and hardly noticed Christopher and Sir Two, if at all. Sir Two marched behind them, with Christopher trying to blend in. Soon they were lost in the crowd that had formed around the march. Christopher was surprised to find that they were in a courtyard of some kind. Magnificent marble buildings circled its center, and in the courtyard surrounding it: a crowd of trees. There were maples and birches, oaks and hemlocks, walnuts and beeches. Thin, tall, some with their crowns more intact, all gathered around a podium from which a powerful voice emanated. The trees were entranced, occasionally cheering in unison. He gazed up at their tallness. They towered above him on the paved ground. So many trees, most simply dressed, all cheering and attentive to the assembly. Christopher's eyes had still not completely adjusted to the light. He hurried, frightened, to follow Sir Two and dared not lag even slightly behind. But soon he was completely overtaken by curiosity about the Mystery. These trees were certainly alive. Staring at the movements around him, he wondered, What would make all these trees come alive?

And then, the marching trees slowed and quieted as they gathered in the courtyard. With Sir Two still in front of him, Christopher listened to the hushed crowd and to the commanding voice that began to speak before them.

"My fellow trees. It is good to see you here again. Today's assembly will be brief, as I know many of you are assisting the Polars in the preparations for Herring Day. But might I remind you that we, like the Polars, must also take this season to grasp at opportunity. We must take hold of this season in preparation for things soon to come. . . . " The voice went on, as the trees cheered loudly around them. Such noise and excitement in the air! "We, my good trees, are a breed of many but basically a breed of one, and I say that it is time to seal that oneness as a sign of our unity, no longer different breeds in spirit but just trees, united. This mark of unity that we have so long striven for, the mark to seal our new economy and productivity, is upon us. Tomorrow, friends, I shall introduce Harold Pine, a fine member of our community. He will demonstrate in full the branding process. We will have assistants available for any concerns you may have. We will protect our young citizens and future generations to come through these innovations that we have been talking about for so long. Finally, we are at the threshold of a new dawn. my friends! Finally!"

"Christopher, we've got to get you back," Sir Two whispered. "Head back to the two trees over there on the lawn . . . quickly!"

Christopher obeyed, trying to make himself as small and unnoticeable as he could. This was not difficult since all eyes were looking in the direction of the voice. He could hear Sir Two behind him saying, "I did not know that Pine would be on the scene so quickly! A lot has happened, boy! Step it up!" Then, to himself: "It has only been a few days since . . . oh . . . "

"Seven-Two! Where have you been?" It was another tree soldier, running up to them. The soldier was a she, dressed like Sir Two, in faded blue and polished buttons, looking at Christopher curiously and with some disdain.

"I can't talk to you now, Twenty-Four. I'll be right back. Wait here for me!" They whispered, as if urgently. Christopher sensed changes about them as Sir Two fumbled for the watch and key. It was fifteen seconds before the minute. "I'm sorry, Chris, you can't stay, really, it's not safe to be seen with me now."

"You're right there," Twenty-Four whispered loudly at Sir Two. "We've got to have a meeting!"

The second hand approached twelve, the gust of wind came, and before Christopher knew it the black night was again in view. He could feel Sir Two nudging him forward. He felt branches in the middle of his back, and then back through the trees they went, into the fading wind, the sounds dying out behind them, the forest ahead silent and empty.

"Here." Sir Two handed Christopher a thick stick and prepared the end for a torch. He pointed, "There is the end of the East, and I am sure in that direction you will find Field. I'm sorry, Christopher, but I cannot escort you further. My forest needs me, and things have developed more than we have realized. Now go—and do take care, lad."

The tree stood for a second and then turned, key and pocket watch again in hand.

"But, Sir Two, how will I ever find you again? When can I return? Please, Sir, don't go away forever. Let me help you."

Sir Two thought a moment and replied, "Perhaps I shall see you again, boy. Don't be so sure we won't meet again. You might return better equipped someday, healthy and stronger, unwearied and clear. It is not certain that you will not, for you do have a human brain, and that is a valuable tool. But don't look for me, Chris. You'll find me only when I find you. Now, go!"

Christopher stepped backward, obeying the command, and continued to walk slowly, watching Sir Two in the doorway of trees, wanting to stay, to jump back through the trees! He watched as the Sir gazed on his pocket watch and then disappeared in the light and wind that came forth through the Door. Christopher saw blurred shadows, nothing clear. He stopped and sighed deeply, standing there for a long time as the light disappeared, leaving only the glow of his torch and Christopher, alone.

In the quiet he finally turned and proceeded slowly, continuing in the direction Sir Two had pointed out for him. He looked up at the torch fondly, worrying about the Tall Sir and thinking deeply and with wonder in the silence of the forest. He walked this way for what felt like an hour and then, exhausted, came upon what looked like a familiar wooded area near the field. He kept on and, finally, unable to walk any farther, extinguished the torch completely, covered it with dirt, and lay down against a tree. Pulling his jacket around him and looking fondly toward the torch, Christopher fell quickly asleep.

~ ~ ~

"Christopher Thomas!" It was the voice of his cousin. He shook Christopher's shoulders. "Thank heaven, you're alive and found! Where did you go? They've been searching all the night!"

Christopher was so fatigued that he hardly answered. He continued to lie there wishing for sleep. "I'll go and get the party. Thank goodness, you're found!" the cousin called as he departed. Christopher thought of sitting up. He knew that he should be awake to be greeted and rescued—and perhaps reprimanded. The daylight hurt his eyes as he struggled with heavy lids.

Blinking, he remembered the previous night and the Tall Sir. He tried to sift through his brain, knowing it had not been a dream but wondering what had really happened, and how he had come to lie here. He had been lost and helped back. Yes, now he could see that he hadn't dreamed. No, he hadn't dreamed at all, for there on the ground lay the torch, its burnt end as black as coal.

~ CHAPTER IV ~

BOOT CAMP

Christopher would have put himself through a training regimen, but there was simply no time. The only thing he could do was bring his compass, so that he would be a little clearer on direction. There was no telling how long the boundaries between his own world and that of Evergreen's would be blurred, and he was determined to get back to help Sir Two.

Christopher would have put himself through a training regimen, but there was simply no time. The only thing he could do was bring his compass, so that he would be a little clearer on direction. There was no telling how long the boundaries between his own world and that of Evergreen's would be blurred, and he was determined to get back to help Sir Two.

Christopher headed through the field, checking his pockets. He had a watch with a second hand, a key, his jackknife, a beefsteak sandwich, and three marshmallow cookies. He turned his jacket inside out.

He worried about Sir Two. As he came to the edge of the field and upon the rim of forest, he remembered with disappointment the words that Sir Two had spoken. In all these weeks of preparation he had forgotten them, and they now echoed head. *Don't look for me, Chris. You'll find me only when I find you.*

Undaunted, he continued, following the compass' direction to the Southwest, one hour's walk time, and waited.

And waited and waited. He called to Sir Two in his head, he called to him out loud. He looked about at the silent trees, which stood motionless everywhere. He checked the ground unceasingly for arrows. Nothing. Not discouraged, he continued waiting and searching. He began examining the closeness of the trees to one another, to see where an Air Door might be.

The morning went on, and Christopher kept hoping. He called out loud for Sir Two, but no one answered. He called out again, this time demanding: "Sir TwoThreeFour-FiveSixSeven-Two! I've come back. It's Christopher, and I have come prepared."

Nothing.

The sun came out and then faded. Soon it disappeared above the cloud-filled sky. There was a touch of moisture in the air. A bird chirped.

It was time, then, to try and get there himself. He had a key. He had no idea whether or not it would work, but it was time to try. If Sir Two would not come for him, then he would get to Evergreen himself. He took out the watch, went back to two trees that were fairly close together, and stood. The minute hand was on the five. He put the key into position, a little higher than his waist. Trying to remember Sir Two's height, he decided it would have to be higher. The hand was on the eight. Would it work? He couldn't tell. What had happened in Evergreen since he had left? Was Sir Two all right? Ten. He hoped so. Had Sir Two tried to find him in the weeks past? No, he was probably too busy. Three seconds. Christopher braced himself and closed his eyes. The seconds passed as he turned the key. He looked at his watch. Two seconds past the twelve. Three . . . four. . . . He did not move. It was supposed to be on the twelve . . . supposed to be . . .

The rays of the sun shone down again as the clouds drifted by. It was quiet in the forest. It was so quiet that Christopher thought he could hear the minute hand of his watch moving quietly along. Nothing. He stood with his arm high, holding the key, not moving, now watching the second hand continue. He sighed, looking down at the ground.

And then, Christopher removed the key and turned. Suddenly, he thought he had been punched in the stomach and gasped, his throat choked in the dry of a gust of air. He had dropped his key and found himself sitting on the forest floor, staring at what he thought was a very angry elf that had materialized out of nowhere.

"DRAT!" I hate Door Clearing day! Hate it! Hate it! Hate it!" His posture mimicked Christopher's, bracing himself with his arms behind him, trying to realize what he had run into. He wore a brown suit with red trim, and had black, greasy, wavy hair under a cap. The scalp underneath the bits of hair was pink, like a baby's, but roads of wrinkles in his face revealed his age, engulfing his squinted eyes in their folds. He was thin and angular in some places like cheekbones, bones and shoulders, and thick and round in other places like chin, nose and stomach. The elf had to be a foot shorter than Christopher, but when he stood, Christopher had the feeling he should not be provoked.

"Where's that darned Door? Darn it all! I've got too much to do to be thrown into this place, of all places."

Christopher rose and pointed back to the Air Door.

"I think it's that way."

"Oh you do?" asked the elf, dusting off his pants. "And what gives you the authority?"

"Well, I met some trees in that area."

"Trees! Bah! Trees. As if an elf ever had to be concerned with what trees do."

"Okay. Suit yourself." Christopher answered.

"Good day then!" said the elf as he started away, mumbling, ". . should be practicing tonight. All I want to do is play the flute. But no. Who'll get the herbs for the honeybell healing spell? Oh, Triddleskipf will do it. Always Triddleskipf. No one else but—Hey!"

The elf stopped, turning back to Christopher.

"Are you a human?" asked the elf.

Christopher turned. "Yes."

The elf wrung his hands, then put them down at his side so as not to appear scheming. "I say, young son, what's on your agenda for the night?"

"Today? I'm trying to get back into Evergreen."

"That so? How'd you like to earn some points?"

"Points?"

"Sure. Points. Don't you earn points?"

"No. Well, at school we do, but any points you give me aren't going to mean anything there."

"Right, right," the elf said, touching a finger to his chin. "How about—no. What if—no. Okay, what is it you want?"

"I don't understand."

"I'd like to employ your services, and so I would need to know what you would like in return."

"What services?"

"The Gold Books, of course."

"What Gold Books?"

"In the Evergreen library."

"You'll have to excuse me but I know nothing about Evergreen, its library or what you need me for."

"Oh. Well. The Gold Books in the library have a type of permanent spell cast over them, so we can't read them. But a human can. And I need a shortcut for this darned spell so I can get back to my rehearsals. How 'bout it?"

"Well . . ."

"Just tell me what you want in return. Anything. Within reason, of course."

But Christopher did not have time to answer, for there was a rush of air, and a branch which materialized where he had stood before. An Air Door had been opened, and it was Sir Two that came through. The elf rolled his eyes.

"Sir Two!" he cried out.

"Yes, m'boy, yes! Come now. The Air Door stays open only fifteen seconds."

The elf stepped carefully into the background, watching Christopher carefully.

"Sir Two, I thought you . . . well, I . . ." he yelled through the wind as it began to die down.

"You thought what, boy? Come now!"

Christopher looked at the elf as he stepped toward the Air Door, but the elf had turned and began to trot away, reaching for a large key in his boot.

When he grabbed hold of Sir Two's branch, a chill passed through Christopher's body. He thought he felt the ground rumble, and going through the trees, he left the daylight behind and emerged into a night of chaos, of noise, of the thunderings of war. He still had hold of Sir Two's branch and they ran, crouching, not in any immediate line of fire but running for cover nonetheless. Christopher tried to turn to see the Air Door, a blur of light that vanished into nothing.

As they ran, Christopher saw the courtyard where they had arrived last time was not there. They were simply in a less dense wood. The terrain was rocky, with occasional dips in the landscape. Trees were scattered and few in the distance, and cannons fired even farther away. He could see lights in the direction from which the cannons sounded, and what might be the city, under a sky tainted with a reddish glow.

They ran for a large rock and, finally stopped, propped up for cover behind it. Sir Two carried a weapon of some kind. His eyes were very alert. He was full of energy and excitement and seemed happy to see Christopher. "You're looking fine, boy!" he exclaimed. "Here, sit a second."

Christopher shook his head. He was too excited to sit. Sir Two leaned upon the rock, looking toward the city. "She's blown," he said, "she's finally blown."

"Sir Two, what happened? Was it that fellow Pine who started the war?"

"Oh," the tree answered, looking in the distance, "Pine's just a prop." He turned to Christopher, "It's that monster, Archer. Wants to make us all the pieces of property that we're not. Oh, everything's blown up, I tell you, the whole ridiculous plan is going into effect. He's woven his way into power, somehow. Wants to make us all the same. All his little puppets. He won't get away with it, I tell you that. A few more seconds, son, and then we'll bolt again."

"But don't you have a ruler?"

Sir Two looked back at him, "A ruler? Heavens no, boy, we have the Ruling Party of Seven. And now that he and Pine are in, well, everything's just going to pieces. Now! To that cluster of rocks!"

They ran suddenly toward a grouping of rocks in the direction of the glow of the city. Something heavy landed near them, and the ground shook. Debris flew through the air above. They dove for the rocks.

"We'll hang low here for a few minutes, lad. They're shifting the cannons."

They sat in the shelter of the rocks. Sir Two said, "It's good to see you, boy, glad to have you."

"Sir Two, what's happening?"

"Oh," he said wearily, "it's all going faster than we had planned." He breathed a deep sigh. "You know that Archer is a brilliant man. Brilliant. Wove his way into our governors like a snake. A real snake. He's out for himself, though, himself, Christopher. For his own agenda. Not for us, not for the trees." Sir Two looked up, paused, and continued. "The worst of it is that four members of our Ruling Party are missing. There are horrible rumors about what's happened to them. Horrible."

"What?"

"Something no tree should ever have to face."

Christopher thought about what that might be, when Sir Two suddenly grabbed his arm and began to run. There was the sound of something above them, soaring and descending. They ran in a crouch over the rocky terrain until they stumbled from a great explosion nearby. The ground shook, and rumbling came from the direction where they had departed. They were heading toward the city.

"Do you think we've been spotted?" Christopher yelled.

He wasn't sure Sir Two had heard him. "Keep moving, son, it sounds like they're heading out!"

They ran farther on, carefully dodging any signs of the departing army. They hid behind rocks and terrain often, progressing always toward the city as the army of trees and cannons, which Christopher could now more clearly see, headed in the other direction. At one point, Christopher thought he caught sight of the elf, but the figure was too deft and swift-footed in the dark. There was another quality about the fleeting figure which made Christopher think of that a magical quality, rather than the darkness, made him hard to discern from a distance.

"They start the siege at night. They're camped east of the city. They intend to take it fully within the next week. They head out after a few hours, sometimes to reload, sometimes not."

They stopped for a moment to rest and survey the area, looking at the city up ahead. Things appeared bleak, in disarray, with trees everywhere in motion. The buildings and houses were tall, very tall, and narrow. They were simple and plain, of a material resembling dark clay; with second and third stories, smoking chimneys, and open windows and doorways. Sir Two and Christopher began to walk again as the cannons retreated in the distance.

"Are they really going to brand trees, the way they said they would?"

"Not if I can help it. Problem is, they've been lying to our trees, and most believe what they're being fed. And why not? Archer's a likable fellow, or he was, in the beginning. Really a brilliant tree, brilliant. He started this Arboretum, you know, a place where they grow trees, like a nursery. They did all kinds of research, worthwhile research, into making different species of trees by combining two or more species. And that was fine. It happens in nature, and, as I said, everyone liked Archer as a good tree and citizen. He was a blended tree himself that came to life. Two of my recruits, they're blended trees out of the Arboretum, Twenty-Four and Eighty-Eight."

"What happened?"

"Well," Sir Two continued, looking stern, "not all of the trees in the Arboretum came to life, just as not all the trees in the forest come to life. I think that frustrated Archer somehow, I mean really frustrated him. It did something to him, and he changed, and that change was something a lot of us did not like to see. Wanted to make the trees come to life himself, or at least that's what it seemed. Then he meets this Pine who is a new member of our Ruling Party. Wants to mark all 'his' trees that come from 'his' Arboretum, that's his idea. And, certainly, he created the Arboretum, or the concept of Arboretum, assisting Nature in making trees. But he never shaped or formed the trees. And certainly he never made the trees come to life!"

"But, Sir Two, how could he own the trees? Nobody owns the trees. How could that ever happen?"

"Well, here's where things went wrong, son. Pine and some others got involved with Archer. It's said that Archer offered his brilliant mind to their service in exchange for their 'assistance.' All of a sudden, he's a member of the Party, and now it seems they're uprooting some trees from Arboretum and taking them to Tallaway, and we don't know if they're being planted in Knobscott and Pinetóba; among other mysterious 'plans.' The worst of it is it's been said that those replanted trees, those sleeping trees, have already been marked!"

"And what about the mark?"

Sir Two looked sharply at him. They were getting closer to the center of the city now. Christopher could see trees everywhere, collecting, gathering, some crying, some organizing groups.

"It says, boy, that those trees belong to Archer. And they don't. He's playing around with power, boy, and someday those trees will be more than hurt by it. They'll be waking up to something they won't know to question. They'll just think they've been created that way and believe everything he tells them. You see, when a tree becomes awake, a bell sounds in the Hall of Awakening, located at the center of our city. We have a large map there of Evergreen and the surrounding areas. The map is a central point of all the sensors that run throughout the land. When a tree awakens, its roots trigger the sensors, which light the map. A beeping sound continues, and the overhead bell rings to alert our city crew. The team heads out to the tree in no time, and helps the tree to get uprooted and oriented, taking the tree gently out of the ground, and, when the tree is ready, into the city where the tree is registered and named. The tree can keep its chosen name or the number assigned to it, or both. The tree is then free to tour the city, visit our library or the surrounding forests and towns, and to take as long as it needs. Trees often want to trace their place of origin, to see if they have relative trees awake. You know," Sir Two paused, turning to Christopher, "I'm not even sure that the new Arboretum trees are being made with normal roots, you see, so they can't be detected by the sensors."

"But how can they mark trees that are already awake?"

"That's where the big error comes in, boy, the big error in their thinking, as if making those innocent trees a part in their plan was not error enough. It's very complicated, son, but let me say this. It has to do with our trade of herring and brick, which is how our city is sustained. You see those trees born out of Arboretum have been sent into the herring business, which is the more profitable of the two. And not just sent in, but they're also growing in number and influence." They were coming out of the desolate area now and approaching the courtyard that Christopher had remembered. The lawn was fresh, unscorched. From this point on, there was no damage to the city. They went past the tall, adobe-like dwellings, past rubble and confusion, toward the sound of weeping over to their right. It came from a group of willow trees, standing some way off. "Don't have too many of them here," Sir Two said. "Not much good for war I'm afraid, but they're wonderful designers. It is said that their ancestors helped to design our city long ago."

Sir Two must have been talking about the city they had come upon, and not the clay dwellings they had passed, which had a temporary look about them. Christopher had been looking distractedly ahead with awe, for beyond the courtyard, what he hadn't noticed at the assembly, was a beautiful city of white marble. Marble buildings and posts, the library, as Sir Two had mentioned, other buildings with lettering across their fronts. Christopher wondered if the courtyard floor itself was marble. He had assumed it was concrete. It lit up the night; this white, unscathed rock. In the center was a wide circular building, surrounded by an inviting staircase, and along the doorway the letters spelled HALL OF AWAKENING. The other buildings had similar lettering: TOWN HALL, LIBRARY, and HALL OF RULERS. Christopher's eyes were trying to convince himself that such a place was real.

"Sir Two! Where did all this rock come from? In the middle of the forest?"

"Don't know, son. I'm afraid I can't answer that."

"I'm glad the cannons didn't reach this far!" he said, and then, puzzled, "How come the cannons didn't reach this far?"

"Oh, they have more sense than that. They're preserving the city so that they can take it over. They know they can't ever rebuild these buildings. They're too valuable to bomb."

"Where are we going?"

"To the Front meeting, lad."

"Where?"

"In the library, son. We are the reinforcements."

They walked across the courtyard. Christopher bent to touch the white floor, looking behind him at the forest and primitive houses. How they contrasted with this white stone underfoot, which lighted up the night. He could see where he was going now. He and Sir Two were visible to each other. He felt cool and alert. He noticed the crude lamps that did little compared with the brilliant, abundant rock.

"So there are parts of the plan of which we are still not aware. We won't know what we're getting into by letting them burn our bark, not fully anyway. And the Arboretums, well, they know even less."

They walked up the steps of the library and through a tall open doorway. Christopher did not see any doors as he looked around, not on the buildings, nor on the houses that they had passed down below—only open doorways.

"Our books are made from grains," he continued, "ground and pressed."

"I was going to ask that," Christopher said, for he did not know how to ask about the trees' source of paper and wood.

"Branches that have been shed in the wood are gathered and used for fire purposes, but only those that have been shed naturally." That was all Sir Two said on the subject. It was hard for Christopher to imagine a society that did not cut down trees.

The height of the library was overwhelming. Marble shelves along the walls continued all the way up to the ceiling, and some books dwarfed him in size. They were layered in levels of three, and the shelves were twice his height. Tables were few; chairs . . . there were none. The stepping ladder, leaning against the books in a corner, headed up so high that Christopher had to stretch his neck to see. It had to have twenty rungs! The rooms were poorly lit, with candles burning in posts along the walls. Christopher was surprised at how dim it was . . . musty . . . quiet. They traveled through a series of similar rooms, with walls and walls and more tall walls full of books.

"Seven-Two," someone said. They had entered a backroom, lined everywhere with books, and with a table in the center, and ten trees standing around. The trees looked at Christopher curiously, then back at Sir Two. One of the trees, the one Sir Two called Eighty-Eight, spoke.

"What's with the human squirrel, Seven-Two?" Some other trees mumbled to themselves.

"He's here on a mission," Sir Two announced in a commanding voice. "He has come by the sign of a shooting elf, and I trust I need say no more. Now, may we continue with the meeting at hand?"

The trees were disrupted and began to mumble loudly among themselves. Christopher looked around for a chair. He was somewhat surprised that they were so casual about his presence here. Never before had he stood in a roomful of trees that were awake, trees inside a building, walking and standing with legs, with features, their branches careful and trim and coordinated. Their barks were different, and each one had a distinctive shape and coloring, as people might. The trees seemed more concerned with Sir Two's statement than with anything else at present.

"A shooting elf?" the female tree spoke. It was Twenty-Four, the one they had met at the assembly. "And when did this occur?"

All the trees hushed to listen. Sir Two swallowed and hesitated. "It happened seven weeks today. And I will propose that the topic of the boy be left for another time since it seems

we have other, more pressing matters and plans to execute."
The trees mumbled again.

This must have been taken as an omen, Sir Two's
mentioning "seven weeks today," for there was a minor
uproar, and one tree even cheered. Another tree, who had a
low voice, and seemed older, with darkened bark, long
branches, and many creases about its eyes and face, was
questioning Sir Two for more information. As things settled
down—Christopher still searching for a chair—the trees all at
once assumed chairlike positions around the table as Sir Two
had done in the forest. The meeting had begun, and
Christopher, somewhat offended, blurted out, "Don't you trees
have any chairs around here?" Sir Two motioned Christopher
toward him, but Christopher headed out into the library.

Christopher proceeded quietly, politely, nonchalantly,
looking at the books about him. He was heading for the room
with the ladder. For he knew, although he had not actually
seen the wheels, that any ladder in a library, no matter how
big or small, or what type of library, for that matter, would
undoubtedly have wheels. Practically speaking, it would have
to have them. He tried to appear as though he had great
interest in the books about him, though honestly he did not
just now, for far more alluring was that towering shape that
was intended to roll, and so, too, were the brass-colored
handles along the walls way up high that invited shoving off.

He came to the bottom rung and looked up. He hadn't
realized earlier just how high it was. As he stood at the bottom
now, it was like a path heading toward the ceiling far away.
He began to climb the wide rungs, and clung to the sides as if
climbing a tree. As he reached the third step, he could feel just
how high the top would be. He felt a jerk to the right as he
clumsily approached the sixth rung, grabbing hold of a brass

handle now within reach. Christopher could not help himself. He had to try pushing off.

And soar he did! As soon as he had pushed the rung, and it had not been a fierce push at all, the air from behind blew his hair to the front, the ladder floated effortlessly as if its square wheels were on slippery glass. Christopher smiled, and when he had slowed down, began to climb again. He looked down beyond his feet, then up the ladder's path, then to his left and right. So many books he had never seen! He could smell a scent not unlike leather, and the cool marble shelves chased away any signs of dampness. He was halfway up now, the tenth rung, perhaps twenty feet in the air.

He came to another brass handle; he pushed mightily, which sent him flying out of the corner and down the row of books, speeding too fast this time. He seemed to be picking up speed instead of slowing down. The marble wall at the other end came closer and closer. He was going to crash, perhaps fall from this height, and, worst of all, Sir Two would not be happy, and would be embarrassed in front of his friends. Christopher's mind raced. He tried not to panic. He hoped to slow down, hoped he would not cry out. Perhaps he could jump to one of the shelves. . . .

There was a glint of something approaching quickly. He thought it was a brass handle. He decided to grab it, unsure of what the force would do to his arm, unsure if he could reach it without tangling himself in the ladder's rungs. It was his only chance. He braced himself for the moment when the ladder would pass it. His left hand shot out at the shining gold, and up went his body, up went his feet into the air, one hand holding fast to slippery metal, the other reaching for anything. The soundless soaring ladder continued on without him, gradually slowing without his added weight. He was hanging with both hands from the rung. Now he had done it. He was twenty feet in the air with no way to get down.

Christopher imagined, as he looked down for a foothold, Sir Two walking out of his meeting, completely befuddled, telling Christopher that he would have to go back to "Field," as he called it, because he was ill fit for war. As Christopher hung there, he sighed. The gold handle was smooth in his sweaty fingers. He looked down to the shelf a few feet below, the books coming out to within mere inches from the edge. He dangled and contemplated jumping, trying not to look beyond the shelf toward the frightening floor far below, estimating the borders he might grab in addition to jumping. He feared falling backward if he could not grab them soon enough.

He thought of Sir Two and remembered all that was happening in this unreal place. He knew he could not let this distraction get the better of him. He let his fingers slip so that his toes were that much closer and, turning his body, reached a hand to the border, clinging, his eyes shut, knowing he could not jump down to the shelf without falling. Just then his eyes opened. As his hand strength was failing, he saw another rung by his hip that he had not noticed. Christopher grabbed for it, let go, and reached the shelf.

Safe. He sat down on the shelf, pushing the books in to make room, heart beating fast in his chest. *Whew!* He was quite sure he could climb down by using the shelves and handles, if only to reach the ladder. He listened, but heard no sound. He was rooms away from the meeting.

As he looked down to survey the next level, he turned back to the odd brass handle. It wasn't just a handle for the ladder. It was the handle to a small door. He opened it.

Inside were some dusty, faded gold books. He picked one up. It was much smaller than the tall books on the open shelves. The letters on its spine were still bright; the book felt soft and old. He reached for the book, The Polars and the Willows. He heard a sound, like the steps of a tree, coming toward the room. The tree walked in, but did not see Christopher and walked out, not looking back, his steps quick and nervous. Christopher listened for more sounds, but there were none.

Christopher opened the book and began to read. " . . . the Polars of Evergreen are known to be mute, unable to speak even a quiet roar, but possessing knowledge above and beyond average understanding. . . . " He turned to the front of the book and read the table of contents:

Chapter 1: The Discovery of the Willows
Chapter 2: The Civil War of the Elves
Chapter 3: Hidden in Tallaway
Chapter 4: Knobscott and Pinetóba (pin-a-tó-ba)
            Settlements

Christopher read for what must have been a full hour. He flipped through the book and read with interest. He looked at its back, then at the books inside the door, then at the other books on the shelves. These smaller ones seemed such a complete history of Evergreen. The other titles of the big books on the shelves were no less revealing: The Sport of Herring, The Writings of Sir Tallgood Oak, and Discovering Disease through the Rings. Yet these gold books were different.

There was the sound of a rumble in the distance, like thunder. As he sat looking up in the dimness of the silent library, he heard the voices of the trees in another room, getting louder as they approached. Sir Two emerged, with a pleased expression when he saw Christopher.

"I see you've found yourself someplace to sit, boy."

Christopher returned the book to its place, closed the door, and began his descent, he thought, somewhat skillfully. He heard one of the trees, Eighty-Eight, comment positively on Christopher's agility.

The trees quickly dispersed, and Sir Two seemed hopeful and happily restored. "We've got a plan of our own, son. An awakening of our very own," he said. "They won't overtake us because we're going to get the Arboretums on our side."

"That's a great plan," Christopher replied. The thought of this had occurred to him, and now and he and Sir Two headed out of the huge doorway of the library to the top of the stairs. Christopher almost wanted to stay and read, but he could hear more rumblings, and wanted to assist in any way he could. "Where are we going?"

"To the front, lad. They need help loading slings and guns. The others will head to Pinetóba for rallies, underground ones. That's where most Arboretums are settled, since they assist the Polars in the herring hunting."

"How do they assist?"

Sir Two smiled. "Branches can assist in their reach from a distance in a different way from paws." He paused. "Do you like the cold, son? It's colder there, you know."

"Oh, I don't mind it."

As they walked out of the courtyard and back toward the dwellings Christopher thought he saw a shadow darken his step, but when he turned to see if anyone had joined them, it was gone. They continued on, walking toward increasing sounds and rumblings: The cannons were returning. As they approached the area where camps and blockades had been set up by the trees, he again sensed a shadow, and this time a chill went through him. He turned as Sir Two approached a tree who seemed to be in charge of loading the slings. Christopher looked carefully and, seeing nothing out of the ordinary, turned to catch up to Sir Two who was now even farther ahead. As he turned, he suddenly felt his heart sink for again the shadow was behind him, this time accompanied by a rustle. He realized then that he had not thought to look for a stationary tree . . . a tree standing still and not clothed . . . a tree acting as if it were asleep but really not, having eyes, having features, and all of its *roots above the ground.* It was the tree whose name he had heard in the meeting, TwoNineEightZeroSixFour-Two! Facing him, reaching for him, the one that Sir Two had called Four-Two! Christopher yelled, but just then an explosion sounded. The ground shook, he lost his balance, his cry to Sir Two was drowned in the thundering as trees raced everywhere to fire back at the cannon. He was caught. The reaching branches were all around him, binding his elbows fast. Christopher struggled as he lost his balance in the shaking of the ground. He felt himself lifted higher and higher as he yelled and continued to fight.

A female civilian tree, running to assist the others, noticed Christopher's struggle. He yelled out to her, "Sir Two! Sir Two! He's been betrayed! He's been betray—" He never finished, for branches sought to cover his mouth and tightened against his cheeks. He was high up above the tree now! Caught in numerous, independently moving branches, heading over rocky terrain and away from the city, heading to where he did not know, only into the night.

The wind blew in his face as they sped into the depth of forest, in between trees, the sound of explosions and voices fading behind. The branches were wrapped tightly around his arms and legs, and Christopher sat, able to move only one arm, which he was surprised to find free. The tree seemed to sense Christopher's movements without having to look up. The ground below was a blur of motion in the dark, and

Christopher was bounced and jangled as the tree traveled determinedly. Carefully, he reached his hand toward his pocket, suspecting that the tree would sense his movement. But he moved so slowly that it was lost in the travel. What he searched for he eventually found. Passing over the jackknife, his fingers touched the cold metal compass. It glinted in the half-moonlight, and Christopher looked at it. He squinted, bringing his face near, and caught a glimpse of its metal needle wavering and settling before the tree's branches sensed his movement and tangled around his free arm. He was a prisoner already in the height of a tree.

They were going North.

~ CHAPTER V ~

PINETÓBA

They traveled speedily through the night, through forest, and through wind, which seemed to be created by their running. They passed shapes and shadows of trees, or what sometimes appeared to be trees, and as they did so, Christopher pondered their existence in the forest. Here he was, carried by a tree that was alive. It had motive. Which side of this war was it on, and why? Why were the trees fighting? Why had this tree acted as Sir Two's confidant? Merely to obtain information, he supposed. And now where was he taking Christopher?

They traveled long and far, Christopher gripping his compass all the while, not able to see it but noticing whenever the tree changed direction. They traveled mostly north, though sometimes west when the terrain allowed. The wind had shifted, the air had become cold, and a breeze blew from the west. Christopher wondered what would become of him, but he thought more of Sir Two on the front without him. He hoped his message would somehow reach the tree, and he thought that perhaps it might. The image of Sir Two's fond, trusting face when he had looked upon TwoNineEightZero-SixFour-Two lingered before him. At a dear old friend had Sir Two looked, he had said so himself, and now Christopher was carried in the very clutches of this villainous betrayer! Four-Two was an oak, apparently, but dark in color, and quite solid underfoot, its weight only adding to the speed of a run deft and continuous. Christopher wondered how the trees could see in the dark. He felt, as they passed shadows and branches, that they might crash into something here, stumble on something there. Would Sir Two know where to find him? He looked down at the tree. He hadn't realized at the meeting just how numerous its branches were. They must have been politely concealed, and now they were fully spread, alert and furious with their hold on their prey. Christopher did not feel much fear. He thought he must be of some value if Four-Two had bothered to capture him. He only hoped that he would not be dropped and flung a great distance in this treacherous run. If he could escape, he knew he could use his compass to find his way back to Evergreen. Again he looked down at the tree, busy running, and at the moving earth beneath them. Filled with sudden outrage, Christopher heard himself shout.

"Hey!" He was surprised at his voice, but very angry at the same time. "Where are you taking me?"

There was no answer. The tree continued on steadily, the ground a moving blur, the wind blowing across Christopher's questioning face. He paused, and then, only much louder this time, enraged, shouted.

"Hey!!"

The tree looked up, startled, and before they knew it, they were soaring uncontrollably toward the rocky path. They struggled to free themselves from each other, tangled in midair, speeding forward and down as they both yelled, "Whhhoooooaaaaaa!"

With a hard impact and some pain they hit the terrain.

"Uuuugggghhhhhh!"

"Oooooofffffff!"

Something had snapped in the fall. Christopher had barely missed a rock next to him, but he had hit others, and began to feel the pain in his shoulders and leg. He was covered with dirt, on his clothes, face, and in his hair. The tree, tall and covering quite a span, looked up slowly with his dark, creased eyes and face, and now Christopher did feel quite afraid.

"What's the matter with you?" the tree bellowed, starting to rise. "I ought to throw you over a cliff—if there were one nearby! What do you mean shouting like that in the middle of a sprint on rocky terrain? Are you trying to kill us both?"

"I . . . I'm sorry, Four-Two," said Christopher meekly.

"To you, boy, it will be *Mister* TwoNineEightZeroSix-Four-Two, and nothing less! You've cost me a good branch!" shouted the tree, still rising. He grabbed Christopher's legs and dragged him, for Christopher was still caught in his branches, and the tree was trying to stand, but he was so angry that he had gripped Christopher's legs tighter instead of letting go. Christopher gave a shout, and the tree continued, turning.

"I won't forget that! I ought to feed you to the hungry Polars! And if I hear one peep out of you, that's exactly what I'll do! Do you hear me?"

This was not a nice tree, he realized. Or at the very least, this was a tree to be reckoned with. Christopher was very quiet as they continued slowly on. Four-Two did not pick up much speed: It appeared they were nearing a destination.

In a matter of minutes the temperature had dropped significantly. Luckily for Christopher, his jacket was insulated. He thought of turning it the right way, but since he'd already been captured, he cared little about being noticed. He did not feel the cold too much, even though the air indicated to him that it was well below forty degrees.

This was a different kind of place. There were rough, mud houses where trees lived, as there were in Evergreen, but snow covered the landscape, and the center courtyard of the town, toward which they headed, was made not of marble but of . . . ice? Christopher could not tell. The most noticeable difference was the constant sound of rushing water: A river flowed between the rows of dwellings. There were several bridges running across it, and houses were scattered toward the woods. The water quietly flowed down a slight slope from a courtyard, surrounded not by majestic buildings but by huge, round igloo structures. Above, behind the courtyard, was a mountain. There appeared to be walkways along it, and some open caves. Christopher was silent, taking it all in. What a sparkling, cool place this was.

They were heading to one of the igloos, and before he knew it, they were descending a wide, turning staircase of stone. He was out of the cold air, the gushing water sound had faded, and the tree carried him in front to avoid the ceiling. They headed down a dark corridor of stone with candle lanterns burning along the walls. Christopher moved ever so slightly and felt the sensing, tentacle-like branches tighten in response. Voices could be heard up ahead. They turned abruptly to the right into a room full of trees, and not friendly-looking ones. They were seated in their fashion around a stone table built into the floor.

Christopher was thrown onto the table in the middle of the frightening faces, as Four-Two disentangled him like a knot in his hair. Some of the trees rose, including the one at the head of the table. The tree's eyes looked red, wearied and wild, yet his bark was smooth and light. He was tall and still, his stature not revealing the tension his eyes betrayed. When he spoke, the air became stale and quiet.

"What's this? " asked the tree.

"Some human squirrel of Sir Two's. "

"Really."

The tree Four-Two spoke under his breath. "He was reading Gold Books in the Library. "

The bloodshot-eyed tree became visibly angered. Christopher assumed this was the tree Archer.

"When did this happen? How did they find out?"

"I don't think Sir Two knows," answered Four-Two. "It was an accident."

"An accident. "

"Yeah. The kid was reading them while they were in the meeting."

"He *reads* them?"

"He was reading them."

"Without *magic*?"

"None as far as I could see."

"How could that be?"

Christopher stood up, thinking perhaps he could make an exit, since they were not addressing him. "Uh, hello. I was just going. I appreciate you showing me around and everything—"

Many sets of branches intercoiled Christopher's arms and legs.

"I wouldn't do that, squirrel," spoke Archer calmly. His voice was powerful, like that spoken at the assembly. It was strong and calm, commanding, almost hypnotic, and resonated in Christopher's bones. "What I would like to know is, what has given you the authority to decipher the Gold Books?"

"What do you mean?" asked Christopher innocently.

"You know what I am talking about. Don't try to test me. You are dispensable."

"They're just books. Nothing unusual about them. Except they're very interesting."

"Do you mean you read them without magic?"

"Sure."

The trees exchanged a secret glance.

"Precisely, Four Two. He may be able to see things that we haven't been able to. Oh, that Sir Two. Always one step behind. Didn't even know what he had. Now, we might be able to see things about waking up more trees. A whole army of trees!" Archer laughed.

"Wait a minute," answered Christopher angrily. What makes you think I'm going to help you?"

The tree stopped laughing. "Oh, I think you will. You don't like being thrown into boiling oil, do you?"

Christopher gulped, but he was still angry. "I won't, I tell you!"

"We hope you enjoy your stay here in Evergreen," laughed the tree. Turning back to Four-Two, the tree ordered, "Take him."

Again, Christopher was in Four-Two's hold. When another tree spoke to the head tree, whom he assumed to be Archer, the tree answered, "I haven't decided yet, Crane. He may be of use."

Christopher was swept out of the room and glad to be out of the stale air. They headed into a passageway, through a wall that was pushed open by some trees who guarded the hall. Soon they were heading down another dimly lit hall. He did not understand how the trees could see in such terrible lighting. He thought perhaps he could reach for his jackknife and make a run for it, but Four-Two held him tightly by his arms and legs.

The hallway ended with a cell. A key hung above it on a round, metal ring. The tree reached for the key, quickly opened the cell, and again disentangled a fighting Christopher onto the floor. Four-Two held him back with a branch pushing against his chest as the betrayer exited the cell, slamming and locking the door, scowling at him with large eyes surrounded by dark creases. Then Four-Two disappeared.

Why he had not been searched he could not tell. But then, he had only the jackknife, and what could he do? Oh, Sir Two! I'm no good to you here! He felt responsible for complicating matters, but he would not think of that now.

Time passed. There were no windows in the cell, just dirt walls. He tried to pick the lock with his jackknife but was unsuccessful. The iron bars of the door were too close for him to fit through, and the key was nowhere to be seen. He supposed Four-Two had taken it with him. Wondering about the time, he took out his watch. It was 1:30 a.m., Evergreen time. He realized that at this point, he was actually hungry. He ate the beefsteak sandwich he had brought.

When he had finished, he took out one marshmallow cookie. He had taken only a half-bite out of it, sitting against the bars on the floor, when before he could tell, and with the cookie still in his hand, Christopher was asleep.

~ ~ ~

Christopher could see before him a fuzzy little chick, yellow and soft, sitting upon his hand. It wiggled and sat, stood up again, and then nestled between his fingers. It did this many times. It became so ticklish that Christopher awoke. He was not happy to find that he was still on the cell floor, leaning on the hard iron bars. His cheek and shoulder hurt, his arms were stretched out and stiff, and it was funny: He thought he could still feel the little chick from his dream. . . .

He could! It must have found his marshmallow cookie. As Christopher lifted his cheek from the door and turned his head toward his hand, now outside the cell, he leaped back, for there was the head of a huge, black furry beast with numerous fangs. It was the massive head of a bear just inches away! It had nudged his hand, taken the cookie, and devoured it. Christopher moved back in the cell, losing his breath again as he saw the size of the long, black claws that scraped the floor searching for more. And then in the darkness, behind that black bear, he saw movement: other shadows and glints of claws. There was a whole pack of bears clumsily bustling about in the small space outside his cell.

Christopher was grateful for the bars that separated them. He could not tell how many there were, and, strangely, he heard no sound. No sound at all. There was no growling, no gritting of teeth. The more he observed them, the less afraid Christopher felt.

They were still moving about, the shadows of muscled, fuzzy shapes blending together. They seemed to be searching for a way into his cell. He stood watching them. One in the front suddenly stood on his hind legs to look above the door. How tall he was! Another one stood to look, pawing the lock at the same time. Standing back in the cell, Christopher was not at all frightened. He supposed he should have felt fear, for they were trying to get into his cell. But there was none. And then, as if a collective decision had been reached, the bears busily gathered into rows before the door. The ones in the front stood still, and then one above the other they climbed. His heart beat faster as he watched their paws and now their huge, white teeth gripping the iron from both sides, collectively, pulling and gnawing and shaking the door.

Christopher could not move as he watched the two iron bars being pulled apart. Suddenly, the bears were climbing down, moving about, dispersing, and following one another down the darkness of the hallway.

Wait! Christopher was still stunned, but as he watched the bears disappear into the shadows, he moved toward the opening and worked his body through. He caught up with the last bear as they moved down the corridor. They moved steadily as one unit; Christopher lagged behind for a moment and looked around, wondering where the passageway was that they had come through, and where they were in the tunnels. He hurried again, wanting just to follow them, but he found himself in the middle of the pack. They were all around him, dwarfing him. The voice of a tree somewhere startled him, and he crouched down, still running. It was faint, distant, and he ran with the soft, black fur.

They ascended a stairway, stealing out of the lower level of the igloo-shaped building and into the night. They were running, across a courtyard, past buildings, through shrubs and then trees, and now up, up a rocky hill. Christopher did not stop. He continued along in the running, in the cold air, the warmth of the bears all around, their coats of fur vibrating with their mammoth strides. They went up farther, onto steeper ground; he was reaching for rocks and branches and roots in his path. He never looked up as they climbed, and then the bears were scattering up ahead on flat ground. Christopher stood up, breathing, watching them as they headed toward a pool and plunged, carefully, one by one, into the water. The sky was getting brighter. It would be morning soon. He looked back at the bears as they emerged from the pool, shaking their fur, and did not understand what he saw. In the flowing pool they had washed clean the soot that had covered their fur, turning the water black, and now they stood clean and white, some cream-colored, still shaking and walking about. Christopher was confused. These weren't black bears. They were Polar bears. As white as the snow. He watched the soot in the pool as it swirled around and headed into a channel, which headed toward the cliff. He went to the edge, following the water with his eyes, looking down as it ran, narrow and steep, down toward the buildings and town, cascading into the air. He was on top of Polar Cave Mountain! The one he had glimpsed in a gold book!

Soon the bears were filtering down through the top of the mountain into dens that had openings to the front of the cliff as well. Christopher followed; the bears did not seem to mind his presence as they headed into their caves and settled down upon the floor. He settled with them, watching them, and as the damp fur warmed him, Christopher once again fell asleep.

~ ~ ~

"A fine thing it is to find you here. A fine thing! I turn my back for one moment, and you've gone to the North Pole! Wake up, boy. Wake up! "

When Christopher opened his eyes, he saw Sir Two's face staring down at him. The bears were gone. They were alone in the cave. "Sir Two! What time is it?"

"Time? It's very early, boy. We've—"

Christopher raised his hand to his forehead, "Wow, what am I going to do about the time? I'll be here for days. Well, it doesn't matter now, I . . . "

"Oh, we can fix that. That's not the problem. The problem is they're after you, boy. We've got to get you out of here! They won't come up to the caves, but we can't stay here. How did you get up here yourself? Our reinforcements are here, working the underground to find the Arboretums who can be trusted. It's too dangerous to have any more rallies now."

"Sir Two, there's something I forgot to tell you, back at the library, about those . . . "

"Okay, boy," the tree answered, helping him up with his branches. "You can tell me on the way. We've got to get you out of here—and back—this is Archer's headquarters now. Come, now. Are you fit for travel?"

"Travel? Sir Two, I'm not going back now! Forget about the time and the rallies, I came here to . . . "

"Yes, yes, I know, and that's all fine and good, but it's not safe now. They've found out about you. Now as far as the time goes, we can fix that. But we've got to head to Tallaway, to the Air Doors there, and you can get back yesterday, your time. Then I've got to get back to Evergreen. There's a war on!"

"You don't have to babysit me," Christopher said, ruffled, standing tall and walking to the edge of the cave. He looked out over Pinetóba. It was very early morning. The sun was bright, and all was quiet below. "I must be quite a threat to your fellow trees or they would not have brought me here. And right they are," he turned, "for I am a threat! Sir Two, forget about the fighting. Did you know that if you answer a Mystery, you are granted a place on the Ruling Party?"

Sir Two turned strangely pale. "Why, boy," he said, "where in heaven's shoes did you get such a notion?"

"You mean you didn't know that? Why, I read it in your own library, as plain as the day. And did you also know that by being promoted to the Ruling Party a member of the party is selected to step down? For there can be only seven on the Ruling Party . . . and did you ALSO know that . . . "

"Hold on. Hold on, boy. Wait just a minute. . . . " Sir Two paced the cave, his finger to his lip, his eyes searching the corners furtively. He stopped. "Christopher, where did you read of such things?"

"Why, in the library. I told—"

"No. Where . . . exactly, in the library? In what book?"

"Uh, it was a gold book, a few of them, small. . . . Oh, I know, The Polars and the Willows. I just came upon it while I was . . . I was . . . well I was, uh—"

Sir Two turned very pale. He caught his balance a moment, then came up to Christopher. "Came upon it?" He turned and paced and then came back again. "But those books are blank! No one can read them because there's nothing in them! They're kept around for historical purposes, all the gold ones are, for their covers and bindings, they're very old. But there's nothing in them, nothing on the pages . . . nothing to . . . " the tree trailed off.

"But I read it myself! With my own eyes! And other things. Sir Two, did you know that—"

"Wait! I don't want to know it. It's nonsense, just plain—"

"You're not listening to me."

"Impossible. It's completely impossible. As if solving a Mystery could grant one a . . . a . . . "

"Sir *Two*."

" . . . in a place of authority, why it's just—"

"Sir Two, are you hearing me?"

"Why, it could never be!"

"Sir Two, did you know that the Willow trees can actually, somehow fly?"

"*What?*" And at that, Sir Two spun around and fell over in the cave. It was a good thing that his knees were bendable, for he would have gone straight down.

"Oh, boy, Sir Two! Wake up! Can you hear me?"

"Oh, that's quite all right, boy. Whew!" He put his branch up to his forehead. "Help me up, boy."

And when the tree stood, he looked curiously at Christopher and took a deep breath. Then he said, "But even if it is true, it's a ridiculous idea. For no one has solved any of the Mysteries, and they say there is a great consequence for answering wrong. We never knew the consequence for answering right, so no one has bothered. Besides, who's going to be a ruler?"

"You are."

"Beg your pardon?"

"You, Sir Two. And you're going to get rid of Archer. For good. And that traitor Four-Two."

"Me? But . . . "

"That's the plan, Sir Two."

"But there's nowhere to start, I haven't the foggiest notion about solving any of those Mysteries, and I've got troops to tend to . . . "

"You can leave that to me. Sir Two, do you know any Willows that live in Pinetóba?"

"Hm? No. They're all down in Evergreen. It's too cold up here for them."

Christopher sighed. "Then we'll have to got back to Evergreen."

"No wait. No. He's probably not . . . well, what day is it?'

"Sunday."

"There is one willow, William, who comes up here every other day to make a delivery, a special sprig in Evergreen that is packed with the herring. It must be picked fresh that day, you know. I wonder if this is his day. We can check with the packers."

"Is that William?" Christopher pointed out of the cave to a willow tree who was cautiously crossing one of the bridges. There were no other trees around. He crossed so cautiously that he just about clung to the railing.

Sir Two looked out. "Yes, that's William. Oh, William!" he called down. The willow tree was startled, looking about and then proceeding on, since he had not seen anyone across the bridge. "Oh," said Sir Two, "we'll have to go down after him."

"Wait." said Christopher, his finger to his lip. He paced the opening of the cave, thinking, and then, after his lips had murmured something to himself a few times, he called down the following words:

"William of the Willows, come up to your fate!" William stopped in his tracks, standing still, and suddenly the tree began to shake, at first a little, and then more violently. He arose a few inches from the ground, still shaking, his eyes wide and astonished as he was rising still more, with greater speed, straight up over the bridge. He sped toward the caves, his branches drooped and billowy in the breeze. The willow surveyed the height, looking down with fright. He went over the stream, igloo buildings, and courtyard, toward the mountain, and then up: past Christopher and Sir Two, who were looking out of the cave. Luckily, there were still no trees below, and it went unnoticed.

"Quick!" Christopher ran up through the hole of the den toward the top of the mountain as Sir Two followed him, asking, "And what was all that about?"

Christopher turned to answer, "Backward speech. It said something in the book about the flying willow trees understanding backward speech."

Sir Two was flustered, murmuring to himself, "Why, of all the . . . " as they made it to the top, and found William standing there, shaking, his eyes wide and afraid. His shoulders were hunched and his hands gripped each other. When he saw Christopher and Sir Two approaching, he began:

"F—, f—, f—, f—, f—"

"Yes?" asked Christopher.

"F—, f—, f—, f—, f—"

"What's he saying, Sir Two?" whispered Christopher.

"I'm not sure."

"F—, f—, f—, f—, f—." And then closing his eyes, he blurted out suddenly, "Fly?"

"Yes," said Christopher. "You are a willow, William. And Willows can fly. And because you're a good, upstanding citizen, you're going to help us get swiftly to Tallaway. Would it be too much trouble?"

William looked at them for a long time, back and forth, and then continued.

"F—, f—, f—, f—, f—"

"Oh, there he goes again," said Sir Two.

"F—, f—, f—, f—, f—"

"Is he saying fly again?" Christopher whispered.

"F—, f—, f—, f—, f—." Closing his eyes William blurted out, even louder this time, "Fly?"

"Yes, William, fly!" said Christopher. "The Gold Book says so, and you've just proven it yourself. You can fly, William! High up above the trees, swift and graceful, with those long flowing branches of yours. Why, you don't even need wings! And you won't have to flap much, because it says that the wind is with you. Did you hear that? The wind is with you, William Willow!" Christopher was smiling.

"F—, f—, f—, f—, f—"

"Oh, for heaven's shoes, there he goes again. This will never do, Christopher, never do!" Sir Two was shaking his head vigorously and trying to keep his voice down. "Can't you see, boy? The tree's petrified. He's shaking like a leaf!"

"Shhhhh!" said Christopher, "You'll scare him even more!"

"F—, f—, f—, f—, f—, 'fraid!"

"Oh, there's no need to be frightened, William. There's nothing to it. After all, you are a Willow, and, therefore, you can fly. Remember? All you have to do is jump off this cliff. For a practice run, of course. You know, go once around the back of the mountain, for starters, then come back for Sir Two and me."

Sir Two mumbled, scoffing at the thought. Christopher continued on undaunted. "It's very important, William. Oh, and, by the way, I'm Christopher. See, we've got to get to Tallaway and, well, don't you want to be a good citizen and help your forest? Hm? Don't you know there's a war on?"

William said nothing. He looked back and forth between Sir Two and Christopher, hoping to be excused. Sir Two stood proudly. Whenever anyone spoke about being a good citizen, helping one's forest, and all, Sir Two puffed up with military pride. He was shaking his head firmly at William.

William inched his way to the edge, looking down at his roots with his widened eyes. He stopped and looked over the cliff, holding his branch over his mouth, shook his head, and stepped quickly back.

"F—, f—, f—, f—, f—"

"Yes?" asked Christopher.

"'Fraid," he said simply.

"Okay, William. How about if I go with you? Here, I'll hold onto you here," Christopher put his hand on William's trunk, "and we'll go together. Then we'll come back for Sir Two. How does that sound?"

Sir Two looked worried as he saw Christopher next to William. He surveyed the height over the cliff. Christopher had stepped onto William's roots, asking, "Is it okay if I stand here?" he wondered if it would hurt the tree, and in turn William nodded his head politely, smiling a little at Christopher. Christopher reached for a branch above, but it was slightly beyond a comfortable level of reach. He tried both hands around the tree's trunk, then reached one back up to the branch, since it gave him more stability. William was still shaking his head.

"Just tiptoe to the edge, William and, when I give the word, spread your branches wide. Don't use your feet—er, roots. Look forward to that sky, and we'll just sail on!"

William looked confused by the words, and shook his head with doubt as Christopher nodded his head vigorously. Inching over to the edge, William again looked out at the height of the cliff. When they reached the edge, Christopher yelled out, "Sail on!"

So startled was William at the volume of Christopher's voice that he, shaking, actually fell over the edge, and so awkwardly that Christopher lost his grip. Sir Two ran toward him, grabbing for his jacket, but they were gone; and not forward into the air but down: straight down, over the cliff. Sir Two hung over the edge, horrified, and gasped.

He saw Christopher hanging onto William's roots and William heading southward, head first, his branches flailing. He could hear Christopher yelling faintly, "Up, William! Look up!" And William, hearing this, tried to look upward, but was so taken by the sight of the ground ahead that he could do nothing but look down. Sir Two was in a panic now, too, running along the cliff, yelling down and shouting to himself. Then he stopped, for he thought he heard Christopher yell something else, but it was very faint, and he could not understand it.

Suddenly, William swerved upward, smoothly, gracefully, with Christopher hanging on for his life. They narrowly missed the ground. William's startled expression turned to a smile of delight. His branches extended like wings, as if he had remembered something. He flapped effortlessly and flew, picking up speed, grinning now, as they moved behind the mountain and beyond. Both Sir Two and Christopher had to shout several times for William to come down and land.

William made several circles above Sir Two's head before finally landing. This did not amuse Sir Two. Nor did the fact that they were both laughing, William and Christopher, and Sir Two said that he was not amused. Not at all amused. In fact, he was flustered from running along the top of the mountain after them. William twirled around ecstatically, throwing Christopher high up in the air, catching him in his branches and putting him down again. William danced around on his roots, pouncing, and Sir Two, disgusted, said to Christopher, "Well, I can understand this simpleton, but I don't know what is it you're laughing about? Come now, what is it?"

WILLIAM WILLOW

Christopher cleared his throat, "I'm sorry, Sir Two. William, we do have to go. I just got carried away. I was hanging on the very edge, you know, and it occurred to me, the thing that was saving me from falling . . . I was close to death and hanging by the toe of a tree, and then I realized we were going to Tallaway today, too, by tree, or toe, you know, with William, William Willow and the Wind, and, oh, never mind."

"Well, look boy. I must go back to Evergreen. Heaven knows, we've caused a commotion enough here. I've simply got to—"

"But, Sir Two, what about Tallaway? The Gold Book says the elves live in Tallaway."

"Yes. What of it, boy?"

"Well, namely, the Mystery of how a shooting elf gets its speed."

"I'm not following you."

"Well, might an elf know where it gets its speed?"

"Shooting elf, boy, shooting. The elves that live there in the trees are just elves, but a shooting elf is another, rare matter."

"What do you mean?"

"We don't know where the shooting elves are or how to find them."

"Well, wouldn't an elf know where the shooting ones are?"

"Oh, I don't know, boy. Listen, I've got to get back to Evergreen!"

"Okay, Sir Two. Would it be faster through the Air Doors in Tallaway?"

"Well, no. I've—"

"Wait." It was William. In his hand he held a vine, which he had wrapped round his waist and handed to Sir Two.

"Well, thank you, William, but if it's all the same to you, I don't . . ."

He gripped the vine in his branches and William propped Christopher upon his root. Without further delay, William took off.

And this time with greater power and speed.

~ CHAPTER VI ~

TO TALLAWAY BY TREE

"They're *roots*, do you hear?" Christopher could hear Sir Two yelling behind them. "Trees don't have such things as toes," he mumbled. He had finally regained his composure after the initial departure from Polar Cave Mountain, and now he argued half the way to Tallaway: shouting at Christopher in the breeze how he would have to return to Evergreen as soon as they arrived, that he did not have time for this journey, but he supposed that perhaps it was faster. Occasionally, he added would Christopher kindly tell William to slow it down as he was bearing the brunt of the turbulence.

By Christopher's compass they were heading Southwest. They were high above the terrain. Passing out of the North he felt the change in temperature; the breeze below was warm now, and the landscape was becoming flat and rockless. In the bright of the new day Christopher felt hopeful now that they were going to Tallaway. He wondered how it had been named. An abundance of fir trees could be seen.

William had not let up in his speed; he seemed to go faster

as he became more familiar with flying. He had not lost his wide-eyed expression since he had learned to fly. It was as though the experience would remain new to him for some time. Christopher laughed. *For a while he will be Wide-Eyed William Willow,* he thought to himself. Then he laughed again, saying, "Tongue twisters by the Toe of a Tree to Tallaway with Wide-Eyed William Willow and the Wind."

William laughed, and Christopher could hear Sir Two shouting behind them about the war, and that this was truly a terrible time to be . . . He never finished his sentence. Christopher could not figure out how Sir Two could hear what he was saying. And he *was* thinking about the war. It was all he could think about.

There was a mass in the distance that Christopher could not yet recognize. Whatever it was, it reached up to the sky. There were many of them, like buildings in a city, but dark. They were green. He squinted his eyes. There were too many of them. Straight, tall, gigantic. He could see nothing beyond them but sky.

"William," he called, "What are those tall buildings up ahead?"

William, smiling, answered joyfully and simply in his high-pitched voice, "Trees!"

Trees? They couldn't be. Christopher had never seen such trees. They had to be giant trees. Did giants live there?

"Do giants live there?"

"Giants?" William looked confused and frightened.

"Sir Two! What are those trees up ahead?" he shouted. "Is this giant country?"

Sir Two had been monitoring the landscape below, and looking up he replied, "Redwoods, boy. Redwoods."

As they came closer and closer Christopher could not believe the enormity of the trees or how high above the ground William was carrying them. He looked down as William flew between the huge stalks; they were like flies among giants, gliding through the spacious forest of majestic, ominous creatures whose trunks were massive, and whose branches stretched up toward the clouds.

"Oh!" cried Christopher. "Are we going to land, William? We've got to land."

Sir Two gave a shout as William began to descend, and Christopher gazed upward at the trees which cast shadows that spread too far off in the distance to be seen.

William descended gently. When they neared the ground, he hovered, allowing Sir Two to land first. Sir Two immediately walked about and surrendered his vine to the ground neatly, wrapped like a rope.

Christopher stepped off William, thanking him, while William smiled and walked around. He had never been to Tallaway but had heard of it. Christopher went up to Sir Two and immediately began, "Sir Two, I forgot to tell you what else the Book said, about Tallaway. Did you know that the shooting elves live in the heights of Tallaway? What do you suppose that means?"

"Is that so? Hmm . . . I hadn't thought of that. Could mean a lot of things. Maybe they're up in the clouds. Now, Christopher, I'm heading to Evergreen. I can return you to Field and arrange the time, as I told you, for the Air Doors here are quite different. Or, you may stay if you like. You're safer on this side of Evergreen, I can tell you that. But please understand, lad, I've got to go." Sir Two was examining the trees, looking for a Door.

"Of course," Christopher replied, picking up the vine, slinging it around his shoulder. "Sir Two, what's the difference? With the Air Doors, I mean."

It appeared that Sir Two had found a Door. "Hmm? Oh.

Well, the Air Doors in Evergreen are narrow and limited to taking you to the forest of your world, with the twelve-hour time difference. But here," said Sir Two, looking up at the height of the two trees, "here they're wide. And they go not only to other times Christopher but," he looked at Christopher sternly, "to other places as well."

Sir Two was preparing his watch and key. Christopher said, "I trust you will get me back at some point, then, since I've lost my key. Oh, and Sir Two, I have one more question."

"You've lost your what? Oh . . . all right, boy. Yes, what is it?"

Christopher looked around and lowered his voice. "Sir Two," he said, and a shiver went across his shoulders, "Sir Two, where do the Redwood trees who are awake live?"

Sir Two laughed. "No, boy. Of them there are none. For heaven's shoes, what would we do with them?" He laughed more. "We'd have no room for them in the East, that's for certain."

Christopher was confused. "But why? Why can't the Redwoods come to life?"

"That, my boy, is the Fourth Mystery. And you have just named it yourself."

"Really? Sir Two, what an army they would make!"

Sir Two laughed heartily. "You said it, boy!" William came back over then, to see where Sir Two was going.

"You had better go."

Sir Two shook his head, looking at the watch. He turned the key, and a slight breeze came through the large expanse of the trees. Suddenly, there was a blur between them. It was not clear what was on the other side, but it looked like a blurred view of the outskirts of Evergreen, with a darker sky; there seemed to be a lot of activity in the distance. Sir Two's hand disappeared into the blur, and as he turned he said, "I'll be back for you, Christopher. When you look for me, I will find you." Then he entered and became a blur. Christopher and William watched as the blurry shape ran crouched toward the town. The breeze and the scene disappeared, leaving the tranquility of Tallaway again before them.

"Only four Mysteries . . . Gee, I hadn't even thought to look them up in the book. I guess I forgot. William, do you know the other three?" Christopher was pacing around.

William shook his head.

"You mean you don't know the other three questions?"

William shook his head.

"Does anyone?"

William shook his head.

"Well, if it's all right with you, William, we've got to go up again. Are you game?"

William nodded excitedly. He was not one for conversation, but he seemed to enjoy the excitement. He certainly enjoyed flying.

"How in heaven's shoes are we going to catch up with a shooting elf?" Christopher mumbled as he stepped up onto William's root. "We'd need shoes from heaven to do it!"

William only smiled, ready to fly. Christopher looked up. There was not a bird in sight, just the crowd of towering trees, as if their very own society in the sky.

"Upward, William."

They soared up, straight up this time until his footprint could no longer be seen. Christopher had to remember not to look down, for the huge trees around them made him feel as though they were very high up, indeed. He felt like an insect among buildings, that reached leagues above the ground.

He wondered how they could compete with the speed of a shooting elf. And if it weren't busy shooting, who was to say that the elf would join in a conversation with them or would its secret of speed? Christopher frowned at the thought of this plan. He thought about it and contemplated the other Mysteries as William soared. They ascended on a diagonal now, and not too fast. They coasted this way for some time until they came close to the tops of the Redwoods. William's pace slowed, and now they traveled straight across, weaving steadily between the trees.

They saw no movement at all, never mind the sight of shooting elves. Christopher yawned. The thinness of the air was making him tired. He blinked his eyes several times, trying to shake off the sleepiness. He noticed a small clearing below, with smaller trees. Perhaps this was where the Arboretum trees were being replanted. Suddenly, something caught his attention. "William!"

As William jerked to the right, Christopher held tightly. "That way," he said, pointing. He pointed to something minute that he had seen only for a fleeting instant: a little dark spot upon a tree.

And as they approached, he saw that he was right. It was a small opening in the bark. "There," said Christopher.

William approached cautiously. It was a hole, and they hovered in front of it. "Should I knock?" he asked.

William nodded approvingly. He seemed thrilled at the thought. Christopher knocked upon the tree. After a moment, there was a faint echo, ever so faint. They waited. Nothing. He knocked again, then peered into the hole. He could see only blackness. Then he heard the faint echo again, the echo of his knock.

"Hell-ooooooooowww in there," he said, and was surprised at the sound of his own voice, magnified, as it raced through the tunnel of the tree and echoed along the sides. "I thought these things were petrified."

William shrugged.

"Well, let's move on then."

They started out, and William looked back. He must have heard something echo back in the tree. Christopher was amazed at the trees' sense of hearing, for he had heard nothing. As they flew back, Christopher could hear the faint sounds, too, getting louder and louder as they approached.

It was a cranky little voice.

"Is there a fire?! What! What is it? A fire drill? Are we having a fire drill? Eh? For heaven's boots, who's there? If I find one of you high-rise woodpeckers up here, I'll shut your beak with sap glue!"

"I'm not a woodpecker," replied Christopher to the voice.

"Who's there? What are ya? And whaddyamean coming around in the middle of the day?"

They saw a tiny face in the hole, not quite complete, with a chin and long nose that came forward, eyes that squinted tightly shut, and a red sleeping cap upon its head. It stayed away from the opening.

"Well? Whaddya want? You're no elf. Your voice is too deep."

"I . . . I . . . well, sir, I . . . " he felt so silly now, asking an elf such a personal question. It just didn't seem right.

The face came forward a little, and they could see the tips of his ears pointing up. The elf didn't seem to be able to open his eyes. He drew back again into the tree.

"You've got ten seconds. Then I disappear. Whatsa matter? Somethin' got hold of your tongue?"

"I . . . gosh, I'm sorry to have awakened you."

The elf's lips pursed for a moment and then he said, "Is that what you woke me up to tell me? That you're sorry for waking me up? Whatsa matter with you? Eh? Good day!" And at that the elf disappeared.

"Wait!"

There was silence. Then Christopher said, "I was called by a shooting elf!"

After a few seconds the face hovered in the darkness of the hole once again.

"I see," said the elf, eyes still shut.

"A circling, shooting elf."

"Oh?"

"Yes."

"Hm."

The elf came forward again. He wore a tiny red felt shirt. His hair was black under the cap, and combed neatly against his head. He struggled this time to open his eyes, but retreated again.

"I came here to help Sir TwoThreeFourFiveSixSeven-Two save Evergreen. I am Christopher, the human squirrel from Field, and I'd like to know how a shooting elf gets its speed."

TRDLSKPF

"Hah!" said the elf, "Evergreen. And who's to say a shooting elf *himself* knows where he gets his speed? Hm?" the elf snickered.

Christopher hadn't thought of that. "I . . . well, I just assumed—"

"That's the word that does it every time."

"Well,, aren't you a shooting elf?"

"No, I am not. And if I were, I wouldn't be here talking to you. Which reminds me I am missing a good day's sleep."

The elf retreated again, and Christopher said, "Wait!"

The elf was gone. He did not reemerge. Christopher poked his head in the hole and said quietly, "Please, sir."

"Don't deafen me! I'm not all the way down yet," they could hear the voice come up. "Don't know what is wrong with you creatures, carousing about during the day. It's indecent!" He was coming up again.

"Why should I tell you anything? I don't know you from my left boot."

"Can you tell me any of the other Mysteries, I mean besides the Four. Otherwise, I'll have to go back to the library, and we haven't the time, nor a key."

The elf waited. After a few moments he said, squinting, "What makes your friend here fly?"

"I don't know. What does that have to do with anything?"

The elf snickered.

"Is that the Fifth? What makes the Willow Tree fly? Is that it?"

The elf did not answer.

"How is it that you know more than four?"

"Don't know."

"Do you know any others?"

"Can't answer that neither."

"Well, isn't there anyone around here that would know? Is there anyone around here who asks questions? Is there anyone around here, period?"

"Well, whaddya expect, coming around in the middle of the day! Why don't you go South for that, leave me alone. Oh . . . I'm getting a headache again . . . oh, drat! All the hullabaloo . . ."

"South? Where?"

"Look at a map, boy. " The elf was turning.

"Well, thank you just the same, thank you very much, Mr. . . . uh . . . "

"Elf. Just elf. That's all." The elf yawned.

"Well, I'm sorry to have awakened you, Mr. . . . . "

"Elf, I tell ya. You wouldn't be able to pronounce my name. Haven't met anything but an elf that could plumb pronounce it."

"Try me."

"Trdlskpf."

"You're right."

"Told ya." They could hear his muttering echoes as he descended. " . . . between the woodpeckers and now this. I'll never make it to winter. Going to have dark circles down to my boots for the rest of tarnation. . . . "

"No wonder there's no one around. Well, should we head South? Perhaps we'll just find more questions. I don't know which is worse: knowing all the Mysteries or not knowing. I wonder what is South, anyway."

"Knobscott!" said William.

"Oh, thank you, William. Say, William," asked Christopher as they flew, "I don't suppose you know why it is you can fly, do you?"

William shook his head.

"What kind of trees are in Knobscott?"

"Oaks!" said William.

"Knobby oaks?"

William nodded vigorously and smiled. And off they went.

~ ~ ~

Christopher was happy to find that they landed in the area of some apple trees, for he was hungry. As he and

William landed, however, he surveyed the area to examine the trees. They had flown over some of the clay dwellings that were seen throughout the land, but it seemed that this place too was deserted. He supposed that all the trees had gone to Evergreen to assist in the war. He wanted to be there, too, loading the cannons, but somehow he felt that he had to do something else, and that his involvement in the war would only worsen matters.

"You know, William, if I weren't so hungry, I wouldn't want to pick some apples."

"Pick!" replied William.

"But is it okay to pick them?" Christopher had come to reexamine all of his ideas about trees. Living among them, he was no longer sure of what was normal and appropriate.

William looked at him strangely, then said, "If not eaten, then used by ground."

That made perfect sense. And so, with William's permission, Christopher climbed and picked apples. He had never tasted such apples. He wasn't sure if it was because of his hunger or simply because they were the most tart and crunchy apples he had ever tasted. He wondered what they would do here: There was something surely here, and he reviewed a few of the plans he had dreamed up. He sat there on the branch and looked down at William, surveying the tree and thinking how he would climb down.

"William," he said.

"William turned, smiling inquisitively.

"How is it that a tree would be awake but choose to stay in the ground?" He was thinking of Neddy.

For the first time he saw William ponder seriously. He frowned and then answered: "Up to tree."

It was a good reply.

When Christopher had eaten his apple, he began to climb down, and it was decidedly more difficult than the going up.

"William," he said, and not hearing an answer, went on, "do trees have to eat?"

"Sometimes," was the answer.

Just then Christopher lost his footing. He grabbed for a branch, his foot searched for a niche, and when he had found what felt to be a knot, he put his weight upon it. William cried out.

Christopher was so alarmed that he nearly lost his foothold again. When he found the knot, William cried out even louder. Christopher tried to turn to see what was wrong, but he was in such an awkward place that he could not do so without falling. "What is it, William? What?" he cried, but William went on only louder. Christopher looked down. The ground wasn't far, so Christopher decided to jump.

It was a fine landing. Christopher turned to look at a now pale William who looked back with a frightened expression, pointing. Christopher was so relieved to see no danger that he put his hand to his forehead and leaned back on the tree. But there was no tree. The last thing he saw was William's wide eyes.

And the light. It was now a small hole and getting smaller as he raced head first on his back down a slide through a tunnel. He cried out, his echo meeting that of William's high-pitched, panicked yell that sounded in the distance. The slide slithered and turned beneath him as he gained speed. He knew nothing of what was behind him at the bottom. He could only imagine! He saw frightening things in his head: a lion, a boiling pot! The slide turned upward, he slowed down, and gently, but still yelling into the silence, he fell onto a dirt floor.

It was not completely dark. Light came dimly from somewhere. He stood, dusting himself off. He could no longer see the hole. How would he ever get out? What would William do? He supposed that he would try to get back up the slide. But it might take him all day. He hoped William would wait. He thought of the vine that he had slung around his chest and shoulder like a rope, but there was nothing to latch onto. Oh, what an inconvenience this was! He sighed.

And where was he?

The dim light came from no specific place. Yet it was all around, not lighting anything specifically, but bright enough that he knew he was in a cave. He noticed that the walls were rough and jagged as he approached them.

High above, he could see a rock that seemed pink beneath its black exterior. Christopher examined the rocks more closely, for though ordinary bits of rock and dark in color, something about them glowed. Looking at the wall, he supposed he might be able to climb up to the rock to examine it more closely by standing on the others. As he grabbed one to test its sturdiness, Christopher heard a voice and jumped back. He looked about the cave, turning, for the voice had clearly said, "The herring." It sounded female. It was not at all a threatening voice. But there was no one there. He supposed that the someone was hiding somewhere, or perhaps sitting in the slide. He searched and found no one. Perhaps he hadn't heard anything at all.

He again braced himself against the rock. And again he jumped. For there was the voice. And the rock that he had touched glowed green! The voice said, "The herr—"

Christopher looked around him and then back at the rock cautiously. He rested his hand on it, and as it glowed again the same voice said:

"The herring is best when preserved in sprig of Evermile."

The glow ceased, the blackness returned, the voice was gone.

Amazing! Christopher looked at the other rocks. He reached up, touching another. It turned purple and glowed.

"The Redwoods may reach three hundred fifty feet, but no more," said the voice. And then another. This one glowed blue.

"The rivers of Pinetóba are rich in chromium."

Christopher climbed and climbed, the voices sounding all around him. At each rock he touched a new sentence began, others ended. He climbed up to the top, toward the bright glow of the pink rock. He stopped, waited for all the voices to finish, and then touched it.

It glowed even brighter, a fluorescent, warm pink, brighter than all the rest. Suddenly, the wall shook and moved. Christopher grabbed tightly as the wall swung around like a door, turning into another room, a smaller one with plain, flat-surfaced walls. It was empty except for a small stone table in the middle that was built into the floor. The wall stopped. Christopher paused, blinking his eyes free of the dust. Then he climbed down.

There was an interesting design of colored rocks, bright like gems, embedded in the silvery graphite surface of the table top. There was an arch of seven along the top, four in the center in a straight line, and two smaller circles at the bottom. Christopher stared with wonder and curiosity and was hesitant to touch them. He reached out ever so slowly to the first rock at the top and touched it lightly. Instantly, it glowed the brightest green, and the soft voice asked, "How does a tree become awake?"

Christopher smiled. The Seven Mysteries. His hand moved to the fifth rock, for he had little time to waste. It glowed the brightest yellow and asked, "What makes the Willow tree fly?" He smiled again at the voice.

To the sixth stone he moved. A white glow washed over Christopher as the voice sounded, "What makes the Polar bear wise?"

Christopher paused and then moved to the seventh. An orange glow and then, "Why have the words of the Gold Books been erased?"

Christopher took a deep breath and looked around the cave. He paused. He exhaled, looked down, and touched the first of the four gems in the middle. It glowed blue, and the voice sounded, "Pinetóba flourishes in prosperity of season."

The second glowed red. The voice said, "Tallaway resides in peace, but with current implants from foreign soil."

Christopher paused as a chill passed through his spine. He tried to think, and heat rushed to his forehead. A voice sounded in his head, his own voice. It echoed as he listened. *This must be an information source for all the forest.* Another sound echoed in his mind, too. This one seemed to come from a faraway place. He heard shouts, the sound of an explosion, the sound of something soaring through the air. His vision blurred. He tried to think and to see the cave walls in front of him. His hands gripped the table. He steadied himself to stand, feeling uneasy in his stomach, his face still flushed. Focusing again on the four rocks in the center, he reached his finger past the third and toward the fourth. He could feel sweat break out upon his brow as he touched it gingerly. There was the dull glow of green.

"Evergreen has been overturned."

No-o-o-o!

He had to get back. He had to get out of here. He was trapped! He looked around, pacing the cave, searching for any openings or rocks that he may have missed. There were none.

He would have to go back and climb the slide. There was no other way. He hoped he could get back into the other cave.

As Christopher raced back to the wall he stopped. He looked back at the table. He stared at it and hurried over. Standing before it, Christopher looked down at the two untouched circles. Stepping even closer, he steadied himself. Not knowing what would happen, he lifted his hands and held his palms over them in midair. Then, closing his eyes and hoping, he began to lower his hands. He had nothing to lose, and there was no time for anything else.

When he felt his skin reach the jagged edges of the warm gems, a faint whistle began in the air. It became a wind, coming faster, increasing in current until his jacket began to flap. Opening his eyes, Christopher saw daylight in front, and the blurry shape of two knobby oak trees. It was an Air Door, a way out, and he yelled out, overjoyed. He wasted not a second, but ran straight into it, plunging head first, landing hard upon the ground and leaves, tumbling into sunlight and air that had become brisk. Relieved, he rolled around and turned to see the Door fading, the blurred dark view of the cave disappearing, a soft air blowing at his cheeks. And then it was gone.

He had to adjust his eyes as he stood up and called, "William! William!!" Looking up, he saw William, flying happily around. Christopher was not smiling.

~ CHAPTER VII ~

DISASTER

When they reached Evergreen, it was late afternoon. There was no sound of cannons firing, but smoke lingered everywhere in the air. William flew high to avoid being seen. Christopher was in a panic. He searched below for Sir Two. This was terrible! Everywhere trees lingered, some crying, others coming out of hiding. It would appear that the warring party had already retreated. There seemed to be lots of activity in the center. But where was Sir Two? Christopher did not know where to look.

"William!" he yelled, "Any sign of Sir Two or the others?"

William shook his head bleakly, looking down at his ruined home, Evergreen.

"William, fly to the center, low, by those buildings over there."

They descended toward some brush and the remains of buildings. And then Christopher turned his head.

"Did you hear that? Over there! Look!"

It was the sound of someone speaking. They flew closer, hiding behind shrubs and rubble. There was a large crowd, enormous—all of Evergreen and what must have been Knobscott, too—in the courtyard. An above-average tall tree, of which type Christopher could not tell, spoke loudly and with command.

" . . . and as you know, there are members of the Ruling Party now missing. I know this is of great concern to you. But if we can remain calm and remember not to panic we can all get to work rebuilding the city."

William slowed down, they stopped on a pile of rubble and huddled low, unseen by the crowd. The voice went on.

"Now, I myself am prepared to offer jobs to any of you wanting to help in this rebuilding—today . . . "

"What's he talking about? They just destroyed the city, and now they want to hire the citizens to repair it? Is he crazy? Who is this tree, anyway?" whispered Christopher furiously.

"Crane," William replied sadly, listening.

"Now as you know, the Arboretum trees up in Pinetóba have been marked in order that their wages be given fairly. For, as you know, there have been some problems of late here in Evergreen with identifying certain trees at the time of distribution of wages . . . "

"Not true," said William, worried, "Not true."

" . . . and with our new system, which has worked brilliantly in Pinetóba, we will have no dishonesty and no discrepancies. Incidentally, just last year our production of herring was increased by forty percent! With more of our trees working the waters of Pinetóba, we can only move on to more prosperity . . . "

"But what about the Polars?" asked Christopher to William.

" . . . with the number of your birth clearly a part of your own bark, there will be no mistaking who is and who is not entitled to their wages when it comes to distribution time. We've been through this before. Now we'll be setting up our system in the Town Hall. If you'd like to sign up now, there's time. Otherwise . . . "

The crowd was listless. There was confused silence among the trees. Some moved about. Some listened. Others spoke in small circles.

"As far as the bombings go," continued the tree, "we have apprehended most of the trees responsible for the destruction of the city. As you know, those criminals have tried to demand wages not their own by impersonating others. Those trees have been responsible for a conspiracy to thwart our new Evergreen, and I have been told that this has been an ongoing problem. But I'm here to help."

"Not true. Not true," said William, a tense and worried expression on his face. Christopher was removing his jacket.

" . . . are still at large and will no doubt be captured in the immediate future. Steps are being taken as we speak to apprehend the individuals. Let me reassure you, my fellow trees. I understand and join in your sorrow. We are doing everything we possibly can to . . . "

"LIAR!" Christopher had climbed a huge mound of rubble which he now stood upon and screamed at the top of his lungs, "LIAR!" There was a great hush. All of the trees turned and faced Christopher as he boldly continued, pointing fiercely, *"Liar, liar, tree on fire!"*

"Who is that?" asked the tree Crane, looking behind him nervously at one tree whom Christopher recognized as Four-Two, the one who had captured him. *"What* is that?"

demanded Crane. Four-Two's eyes were wide, angry, as he rose, answering.

"It's the human squirrel."

"He's lying," Christopher yelled to the crowd. "There are no thieves! They bombed your city themselves, and now they want you to be their slaves! Don't do it! Don't listen to him!"

There was a great murmuring in the crowd now, and Christopher could see two trees running off to the right and circling behind the buildings of the courtyard. One of them was Four-Two. Most of the trees looked at Christopher, confused, as Crane continued:

"Capture that thing! He is one of them! No need to be alarmed, my trees."

"I am no thing!" said Christopher to Crane and then, turning to the trees, he continued, " I am the human squirrel, called by a shooting elf and sent to Evergreen to call you to revolution!"

Now there was confusion everywhere. All the trees murmured loudly and moved about. Crane called behind him to some other trees, and, suddenly, Christopher saw movement to his left. He turned, and there behind him scrambling up the rubble ran two evil trees, grimacing at him with branches outstretched and fast approaching.

William gasped and soared toward him as Christopher was seized on all sides by the branches. There were shouts and cries from the crowd as they saw William take off. Christopher was far away.

"Look! Look at the Willow!"

William flew as fast as he could as Christopher was slashed with the fury of branches from the two trees. "Oh, no, you don't!" Christopher yelled, fighting. They fought on top of the rubble, slipping on the bits of debris. There were more gasps from the crowd as the trees slipped and pulled

Christopher's fighting form down with them amid the whipping and lashing.

"Seize him!" ordered Crane. "A criminal!"

"William!" Christopher yelled, grabbing a tree's branch and snapping it as he pushed the trunk of the other with his foot. The more he fought, the more he was whipped and coiled. The trees were regaining their footing. The crowd was in chaos as Crane tried to continue to calm them.

Suddenly, Christopher felt two branches latch around his ankles. He was being hoisted in the air. It was William! The two trees were tangled all around Christopher and soon they were all being lifted over the rubble. One tree freed himself. The other, Four-Two, hung on as Christopher tried to get loose from his grip.

William flew erratically over the crowd, which now screamed below. "Isn't that William Willow?" someone cried. He was trying to shake Four-Two from their grasp. And now Four-Two, feeling himself loosened over the crowd, looked up at Christopher with his dark eyes. Christopher could feel the tree's coarse bark tightening around his skin and ripped clothes. With a smile, Four-Two stared into Christopher's eyes as he squeezed tighter. Christopher felt his skin begin to tear as he stared back at Four-Two. With the same sinister smile, Four-Two brought forth a thick branch, lifted it to Christopher's face, and slashed his cheek deeply. As they flew toward the podium, Four-Two jumped. The crowd screamed as Four-Two was caught in the branches of the crowd and fell to the ground.

"After them!" yelled Crane.

William flew swiftly behind rubble and out of their sight, taking sharp turns and flying with such speed that he could not be followed. They were, indeed, being chased, and they continued to the outskirts of Evergreen. For William knew that Christopher was not ready to leave Evergreen. Somehow, although he did not understand why, he knew. And so he continued on this way, until they were far and seen by no one.

"Thank you, William," said Christopher. Blood from his cheek dripped down his face and neck.

William was troubled. "Sir Two not here," he said simply to Christopher as they landed and Christopher stepped down.

"Oh, I know that, William," he said. Christopher was ripping the sleeves from his shirt, which was torn to shreds. He used them to wipe the blood from his cheek, neck, and arms.

William shook his head, still confused.

Christopher removed his vine rope, which also had been torn. He knotted it together and hoisted it back around his shoulder and chest.

William paused. He let out a breath as if he were going to speak. He stopped and then started again:

"Then we . . . leave?"

"William?" said Christopher, tying a ripped piece of shirt around his head.

William listened eagerly, a worried expression in his eyes.

"We're going to wake up the Willows."

There had been no Willows at the rally because, as Sir Two had said, they were not much for wars. In fact, the Willows had retreated to the forest as the bombings increased. They were a shy and reclusive breed, often staying amongst themselves. It was not long before they came upon a sad group of about fifteen Willows.

Some were weeping.

William did not shout, he did not speak, he did not land. He merely flew. Flew around them and between them, joyous and triumphant, as if carrying great news. They did not notice him at first. Then two trees looked up at him, and in their shock dropped what they held. Another willow stood pointing. Still another whispered, "William?" William flew for a long time among them, laughing at first and then saying loudly and clearly, much to Christopher's surprise:

"Fly! Fly! To your fate, fly!"

They rose shakily, as though controlled from without. They flew as a group a few feet in the air. Some rose higher, unsure of what to do but slowly ascending, a branch flapping here and there. Others just stood in amazement, staring at the ground, shocked that they had risen a few feet. A few still stared at William, unaware that they had left the ground.

"Fly! Fly!" cried William.

Soon all of the Willows were flying about, most of them both thrilled and afraid with a happy fright. Christopher smiled at their faces as they floated. Here was such a melancholic breed of tree, he thought, and for such a thing to happen to them. . . . Perhaps they had been weeping because they had forgotten how to fly.

"William," said Christopher, looking around, "Gather the trees onto that rock over there. We've got to organize them."

William nodded, understanding.

And, indeed, it took some organizing to get the trees to land. Christopher had to shout out, "Trees! Trees! Please, there's a war on! We need your help!" This call seemed to help, and as Christopher explained their predicament, the Willows became more serious and attentive. Their faces were solemn again, and they seemed to believe Christopher's every word. There was a trust that he could not identify, as if the trees would do whatever was asked of them, so grateful were they for being liberated. But he really hadn't done anything at all, it had been William, and he put them in William's charge.

The plan was established. They would go to Pinetóba, where Sir Two was surely being held. They would sneak down from the North side and enter from the East, setting up a base on the outskirts.

"Then I will proceed down to the underground to find Sir Two. William, you know what to do from there, right? Now, William, are you sure it's possible?"

William nodded.

"Okay. Then on! Quickly!"

They soared off through the air of twilight, William leading, as Christopher hung on, leaning, searching ahead. Christopher could hear Sir Two's voice. It rang in his mind several times. He tried to push it away for now. He kept his eyes searching ahead and below.

Something no tree should ever have to face.

"Yes, William," said Christopher, "as fast as you possibly can fly."

~ ~ ~

It was night when they reached Pinetóba, and the first thing that Christopher noticed, besides the burning lamps around the town, is that it was heavily guarded.

It had begun to snow. It was a light, fluffy snow. There was not much wind. The large flakes fell softly around the trees, into the flowing stream, and onto the igloo buildings that reached up to the Polar Caves. Christopher proceeded through the wooded area where he had left the Willows, checking his watch to keep track of the time. He came to the rear of the courtyard and eyed the building he had been led to in his own capture. He crouched down against a tree and then stood abruptly. This was confusing in the dark! It was terribly racking upon the nerves, this business of wondering whether or not a tree was awake. He would have to watch a tree for several minutes to make sure that it was asleep, and after all that he was still not too sure. Some of these trees did not appear to wear uniforms, or what they wore was dark and dull. He decided to stick to shrubs and large rocks as he neared the courtyard.

Christopher nearly tripped upon something on the ground. He thought he had been seen by a tree who quickly turned around. He kept still and dared not breathe. How was he going to cross the courtyard? He crept alongside one of the buildings, his heart beating fast at every flicker of light, the snow falling softly around him.

Then he saw it. There it was, the doorway that led underground. How would he make it there? He saw two—no, three—moving trees. They could easily turn, and he would be caught. There was no place to hide. Christopher's heart sank. There was just a big, open space between him and the doorway. There was no way around it: He could see more guards in the other direction. He could not stay where he was for long because the guard trees kept turning about. His heart beat faster. He would have to make a run for it.

He waited several minutes for the guards' backs to be turned at the same time. Then he ran. He ran as quietly as he could, as quickly as his feet would take him. He did not stop. He did not know if he had been spotted on the other side or even if he was being chased. The only thing he could hear was the wind in his ears. He looked at the door that led down to the caves, fixed his eyes upon it and kept running. Suddenly, he remembered something about the courtyard, something that he had forgotten.

It was a sheet of ice.

Because of the snow he had forgotten this detail. His feet slipped slightly. Since the doorway was getting closer, he decided it might be best to simply stop running. Instead, he slid at great speed, fearing that he would crash and tumble down the stairs. He reached the doorway, grabbing the sides, and crouched inside.

The guards continued to pace, and Christopher descended a few stairs, his back and hands against the dirt wall. He had not been seen! Impossible! He caught his breath.

The staircase turned. He watched the flickering candles beneath and felt his face wet with melted snowflakes. For a moment his cheek stung. Remembering Four-Two made him all the more determined to continue down the stairs. Just then he heard voices.

He stopped, frozen, the voices coming closer as two trees approached below and passed by in the corridor. They continued down the hallway and were gone. Quietly, Christopher exhaled. He could feel his palms sweating and the dirt from the wall sticking to them as he came to the bottom of the stairs. He looked to the right and to the left. He heard faintly another single voice coming down the corridor from a distance, disturbing in its tone, arguing. It was a voice that he did not like.

He went in the other direction, searching the corridor, heard a guard approaching, stopped, and ran back. There was a crevice in the wall into which Christopher barely fit. As he hid, watching for the guard, he heard the angry voice again. It was louder.

"What do you mean by that, Sly? We'll use them as an example, what else? We need to have an example of what happens to a good citizen who does not obey its rulers."

"But we can't keep them around forever. Evergreen doesn't have any prisoners because Evergreen doesn't have any crime."

There was a sudden chill in the air, an uncomfortable pause. Christopher listened for more sounds.

"I am going to act as if I did not hear that, Sly. Sly, I am going to give you another chance. For we know that Evergreen does, indeed, have crime. It certainly does have prisoners. I can show them to you if you like. I can even make you one of them, Sly, if you prefer. But I warn you of that because I said nothing of keeping them around forever. No, I don't recall that. Do you, Crane? I think those were your words, Sly, and do you know what? I'm tiring of hearing you talk."

There was a pause, then a low voice began.

" . . . I'm saying is that the missing rulers were one thing, but, publicly, we can't . . . I mean . . . the trees won't—"

"They won't what? They won't follow along? Haven't they followed faithfully this far? And when they see for themselves these examples of depravity, the outcasts, well . . . "

"But—"

"What could be worse for a tree, asleep or awake? Could there be anything worse than . . . fire?"

No! Seeing the guard disappear, Christopher ran away down the dark corridor.

There was a solid iron door at the end of one of the corridors. As Christopher approached, he heard more voices. He thought he heard Sir Two's voice. Yes! It was Sir Two! He ran to the door and stood on his toes to peer through the tiny window. There was Sir Two with about ten other trees. They were huddled in a circle, whispering.

"Pssst!" said Christopher through the door.

"Who's there?" said a voice.

"Shhh! It's me, Christopher."

"Christopher?" came back a whisper. "Boy, how did you get in here?"

"I ran," Christopher said.

The trees murmured within. Sir Two tried to hush them. Christopher looked up. There in the darkness he thought he saw the glint of something hanging up near the ceiling.

"Boy, what are you doing? Go now—before you're caught."

Christopher heard the sound of a tree walking down the hall. It was getting closer. There was nothing to hide behind: Christopher could only crouch in the shadows of the corner.

The footsteps stopped. Christopher held his breath. Then slowly, step by step, they continued down the hall.

"Boy, don't worry about us, I tell you. Leave this place at once! Here, I'll give you my key. Take it to the Redwoods, and—"

"No." Christopher said, holding back his emotion. He remembered his jackknife, safe in the pocket of his pants. He removed the vine from his shoulder, took the jackknife and tied it to the end of the vine, and flung it up to the key ring near the ceiling. It linked, caught, and came clanking down to the dirt floor.

There was a murmuring in the cell. Christopher put the key ring and the knife in his pocket, came to the cell window, and said, "Sir Two, in precisely thirty-five minutes this door will be opened, and our revolution will be rescued."

"What do you mean, lad, you've got the key, don't you? Open the door."

"If I do that now, we'll only be captured again. We have no means out of here. There are guards everywhere," he whispered. "Now, listen, set your watch, instruct your men to follow whatever instructions William gives."

"William?"

"Sir Two, give me your word!"

There was a pause.

"All right, boy. Where to?"

Christopher strained to reach the window. "Do I have your word?"

A pause.

"Yes, you have my word. What's happened to your face?"

"Good," Christopher said, and looking at them he added, "Get ready for the reinforcements."

Christopher stole down the hall, looking both ways at each turn. He could see the stairway to the courtyard and went swiftly toward it. He felt hopeful that he could make it back. As his foot met the second step, he began to run.

Checking his watch, he could feel the night air and see the falling snow as he neared the top. There were two guards in sight in the courtyard, and he felt his legs weaken. He waited for the guards to turn. He thought he saw a shadow below. He waited and listened for any sounds. Then, as the guards looked the other way Christopher ran, this time toward a bush in the direction of the woods. He slid along the ice and dove for the bush.

Christopher crouched silently after rolling over. He watched the guards closely and kept perfectly still for a few minutes. Crawling and then running, he made it into the woods.

When he reached the Willows, they were standing and ready. Christopher was out of breath. He gave William the key, saying, "You're sure you can fly through those tunnels? Are you sure? You know what to do. I'll be waiting for you."

William was shaking his head. He was slightly nervous, but he seemed more confident than before. The Willows stood behind him.

"Down the staircase and to the right, at the end of the second hall is an iron door. There are eleven of Sir Two's men, er, trees. It's up to you to reserve the remaining Willows for a distraction, if it comes to that. By my watch they will expect you in precisely sixteen minutes. The guards are everywhere, William. You'll have to fly high and then move in from there." Christopher knew that the Willows would not be armed, but the speeds they could reach when flying were such that they would be like powerful aircraft, too swift and forceful to be stopped by anything in their path. Besides, the trees could only be damaged by gunfire, not destroyed.

William nodded. Christopher felt confident that they could succeed. As he ran up the rocky cliff, he turned and saw William leading the Willows out of sight.

~ CHAPTER VIII ~

MYSTERIES IN THE SNOW

Christopher climbed steadily as the snow fell upon his flushed cheeks. He was not tired. His heart raced him on, up the slope as fast as he could go, slipping occasionally as the snow gathered on the rocks and dirt. He had not gone far when he could see the Polar caves ahead.

When he reached an opening to the cave facing out over Pinetóba, he was cautious in entering it, looking down over the town, down at the lamps, at the guards scattered everywhere. He saw no signs of William or the Willows. Upon entering the cave, Christopher was sheltered momentarily from the weather. He began to climb up through the den to the top of the mountain. As he came up through the hole, he looked around. The snow fell silently into the pool of water and melted. Where were the Polars?

He wondered. He poked around through the other dens, careful not to be seen from below, and did not find a single bear. Coming upon the last cave, he thought he saw something small and white. As he went down through the den, Christopher smiled as he looked upon a small sleeping cub. The cub looked so peaceful that he did not want to wake him. He stood there watching the fuzzy fur, the little breaths that heaved quickly in and out, the wet, black nose that twitched occasionally, the eyes that were closed in sound sleep.

Poor little fellow, Christopher thought to himself, *Did they leave you behind?*

The black eyes opened and looked at Christopher, at first blinking sleepily and then they staring at him with a quiet familiarity. The cub lifted his fuzzy head, and into the small, black eyes Christopher stared in amazement. It was as if this cub knew him, had waited for him, and spoke with his eyes. The cub rose, yawned, stretched, and then shook his head and body right down to his tail. With a twitch, he turned to look at Christopher and walked out of the den.

Christopher followed. They walked out on top of the mountain, by the pool of water, through a bit of shrub, and then out to a clearing. Christopher followed the cub all the way to a shaded area of trees, lit by what had to be moonlight. They walked in the snow to a covering of rocks and dry ground and there, in groups of white fur, sat the Polars.

For the first moment Christopher felt a little frightened among them. He had not quite been invited here as he had the last time . . . or had he? Some of the bears looked piercingly at him with their warm, moist black eyes. He felt a sudden heartache for the creatures that lived in Evergreen. Here, they lived peaceably among the trees, separately but as a part of the community. And now everything was changing in Evergreen. Who could tell what Archer would do? Would he be so horrible as to harm these beautiful bears? Christopher looked sadly upon the faces, at their moist eyes that stared back. His eyes filled with tears at their silence. The bears were so innocent, and yet it was as if they knew, felt the changes, knew Christopher's very thoughts. *But what can I do? I can't help you. I've done nothing to solve anything so far. Sir Two and the Willows will be here if all goes as planned, but then what? I don't know what to do. We're certainly outnumbered.* Christopher sat upon a rock, overwhelmed with confusion, with hopelessness, and with sorrow at the plight of these beautiful, silent creatures that sat peacefully in the snow. Not knowing their fate, away from the mess and confusion. Harming nothing around them.

The snow. It had stopped snowing. As Christopher looked up from the ground at the air there were no more flakes. He turned to see the bears walking away slowly and steadily in the moonlight. They paced along, Christopher with them, heading he knew not where, except that it was away from the Polar caves. The air was cold, and he felt chilled and confused. He stopped as the bears began to disperse, walking off in different directions. He didn't know where or why, but they were disappearing into the night. Discouraged, Christopher headed back to the mountain. He checked his watch and began to run. When he reached the mountain, he ran past the pool and over to the edge.

William Willow was right on schedule.

It was a sight! Below him, emerging from the underground like stalks of celery and flying through the air were the Willows, carrying Sir Two's men. Head first they came and soared up into the night, pursued by a confusion of guards.

When William and Sir Two reached the top of the mountain, Christopher could hear Sir Two's loud voice. "You did it, m'boy! Hah! You've done it! Why, this is the greatest escape I've seen yet! And these Willows, why, I didn't know they had it in them."

As the other trees followed and landed Christopher asked solemnly, "Sir Two, may I borrow William?"

"Sure, boy, sure," said Sir Two, "By all means."

"And in the meantime, maybe you and the rest of the troops should head to Tallaway, to plan for the morning?"

"Right, lad. And don't look so glum! What a victory!"

He trusted that Sir Two would organize the party as the guards climbed cautiously up the mountain, not really wanting to come up to the Polar bears' turf. And that is exactly what Sir Two proceeded to do.

"William," said Christopher, stepping up and pointing, "this way."

They flew back in the direction of the Polars, high in the cold air, the moon shining now like a spotlight in the sky. They flew without speaking. William thought about what he had just accomplished; Christopher tried to figure out what in the world they were going to do next. William flew higher, and Christopher, looked down and said, "Higher, William."

They flew up and up until the air became thin. "Back now, circle back," Christopher said, looking down eagerly. He yelled suddenly,

"Stop!"

William hovered, the wind whistling past them through the cool night air.

And there below Christopher saw something his eyes could at first not believe. William, too, looked confused at the sight, and Christopher did not think that William understood. For there in the sparkling snow, far, far below, imprinted upon the white landscape in the dark of night, lit up by the brightness of the moon, were the words that he had been seeking. Here it was, written and clear, in words large and few, penned by silent paws, by the bears that Christopher could now see, walking below and to the right. Collectively, solemnly, and steadily they moved away. And so apparent now. . . . Christopher stared a long time, not speaking, stunned, watching the bears as William hovered there in the cold.

After a few minutes he heard William's voice.

" . . . to Sir Two?"

"Hmm? Oh. Yes, William."

He hardly noticed the few, scattered flakes that had appeared again, falling plump and light around them in the moonlight, sparkling down into the air, wavering softly and landing evenly upon the ground. They fell into the prints of paws below, erasing the word from Christopher's view. He was so stunned that he had barely noticed the snow, now falling thickly and heavily as they moved on toward Tallaway, descending from the heights of the sky and toward a warmer air in the blackness of night.

"What's that?" said Christopher as they flew over the Redwoods. There was a fire below, what looked like a small campfire, and as they neared the burning light they could also see the trees, smoke, movement, and . . . did he hear music? As they descended he realized that the music came not from below but from the heights of the trees; Christopher looked above them and as they floated down it faded in pitch. They landed.

They were greeted with a cheer, and someone gave Christopher a large plate of smoked herring. The trees were joyous but anxious. They were deep into their planning.

"We have a chance, and that's all it takes," said Sir Two as he approached.

At that, they walked, Sir Two with a torch, Christopher with his plate of herring, which he ate along the way. He tried to talk between mouthfuls, but Sir Two would not have it. When Christopher had finished eating, he asked, "What have you planned for tomorrow?"

"Well, we've got to organize the citizens of Evergreen. Have a rally first thing, at daybreak. Then . . . "

"Sir Two, I have the Answer."

"Well, first, hear my plan, boy."

"I'm not talking about a plan."

"Well, if it's a speech you want to present . . . "

"I don't have a speech."

"A secret weapon then?"

"No."

"Well, what is it, lad?"

"I have the Answer. The Answer to the Mysteries."

"Is that so? Well there are Seven of them, boy. Which one do you have?"

"All of them."

"All of them? That's impossible."

"Hardly."

"And how did you come to this Answer, might I ask? You know there are grave consequences for answering wrong."

Christopher paused. "I will say that I did not come to the Answer by my human brain . . . not completely . . . I guess something else led me there. To the thing that was obvious, but seemed always hidden, and then . . . well . . . then it was told to me."

Sir Two was silent. Christopher looked up at him, his face lit by the light of the torch. "Sir Two, it's up to you, and your friends, to save and rule Evergreen."

They were quiet. Then Christopher said, "It is the one Answer that answers all of the Seven. I wondered myself which one it applied to, until I realized that it applied to all of them. And that means that you and six of your best in command will have to step up."

"If the Answer is wrong, boy, then do you know what happens?"

"No, I don't remember reading that in the book."

Sir Two was silent.

"What? What is it?"

He was silent still.

"What?"

Sir Two looked up at last and said, "We become asleep again, lad, never to awaken again."

Christopher was quiet. He hadn't read that anywhere. He paced around. Then he searched the ground for a large stick. Coming back, he said,

"Sir Two, I'll give you the Answer, and then you can decide. I certainly can't stay here. It's up to you. If you want to keep making war with Archer and his men, well, then that's up to you, too. But sooner or later things are going to have to change. And they're not going to change with that monster where he is. Can't you see that your destiny has changed? You're still a soldier, Sir Two. Always a good and true soldier, and forever will it be. But you're a ruler now. You've got to accept that. You've just got to. If you don't, things will keep getting worse. Are you hearing me, Sir Two? It is willed that way. *The Ruler Unseen has willed it for the good of all.* That's the Answer. It's too late for war. It's too late for anything else."

Sir Two was quiet.

"Here, kneel."

Sir Two knelt before Christopher. Christopher tapped the stick on Sir Two's shoulders.

"I, Christopher of Field, dub thee, Sir Two, carrier of the Answer and Ruler of Evergreen, for his acts of excellency and his mightiness of deed."

~ ~ ~

By the time they reached the campfires, Christopher had filled Sir Two in on his adventures. Sir Two listened intently as he relayed the story of the public rally and how he and William had escaped. Sir Two seemed delighted at all the details, and at times they laughed mirthfully.

"I am sorry he scratched you, that's quite a gouge. I'm so disappointed in Four-Two, we had no idea, and had our hopes in him," Sir Two reflected. "Yes, he can be a nasty one, that Crane can . . . " and then, "Did you *really* call him a tree on fire?"

As they readied to leave before daybreak the next morning, Sir Two asked Christopher, "Do you realize that although we can travel to Evergreen by Air Doors, we'll have to fly back to Tallaway in order to return you to Field by the proper time?"

Christopher thought a moment and realized that he was right. "Oh, well," he said. And as Christopher filled Sir Two in on the remaining Four Mysteries, the tree soldier Twenty-Four came up to them and said, "The troops are ready." She looked at Christopher and added, "You're okay with me, kid," and departed.

Sir Two stood by until everyone had passed through the wide Air Door of the Redwood trees and into the desolate forest of Evergreen. All was quiet with the new day. They marched steadily through: Sir Two, William, and Christopher in front, Twenty-Four and Eighty-Eight directly behind, followed by the rest of their troops.

They continued on their march through the rubble, the smoldering ground and piles of debris, to the center of town. They knew there would be much activity there. A multitude of trees filled the town. Trees of all kinds, but mostly oaks, spruces, and maples. The crowd was even bigger than the one they had seen yesterday. It formed an enormous line, twisting and turning through the courtyard and spilling over to the outskirts.

Sir Two led his group right into the line, cleared his throat, and innocently asked the tree beside him, "Excuse me, my good man, but to where does this line lead?"

"To the jobs," said the tree, as if Sir Two should have known.

"That's right, that's right! Step up, my good trees!" came a voice from the front.

"Sir Two . . . " said Christopher.

Sir Two was looking at the crowd.

Twenty-Four poked from behind, "I say we storm those traitors!"

"Calm it," said Eighty-Eight.

"I wish I could just talk with them first," Sir Two was looking up ahead, " . . . make them listen."

"We've done enough of that," Twenty-Four whispered. "Look who they're listening to!"

"She's right," said Eighty-Eight.

"Sir Two, we've got to get to the Hall," said Christopher.

" . . . if I could just reason with them once more, if . . . " he was looking over the trees toward the front.

"No! We've got to act! Come on! The plan! They'll only put you away," said Twenty-Four.

Sir Two moved through the crowd, followed closely by Christopher and the rest of the troops. The voice up ahead talked on; the crowd murmured around them. Sir Two moved swiftly now, and Christopher stayed right with him, worried that Sir Two was making a detour on their way to the Hall of Rulers. They approached the courtyard center, where, among many Arboretum trees, they could see trees from the line approaching timidly the doorway of the Town Hall. A large machine blew steam and hissed. Trees were walking away from the building holding papers, and Christopher squinted to see what appeared to be a small bit of darkness upon their barks.

"Stop this!" Sir Two ran into the courtyard. "Stop this at once!"

"No!" said Christopher, grabbing Sir Two's lower trunk in an attempt to stop him. Sir Two ran on, dragging Christopher, who clung to his leg. Christopher thumped along over the hard surface and the roots of trees in his path.

Archer then spoke. He looked at Sir Two, startled, and immediately ordered, "Criminal! Seize him!"

"*Oof!*" Christopher had lost his grip, and Sir Two had jumped up onto a table as guards began running through the crowd toward them.

"My fellow trees! I am no thief. Please, don't do this. You've got to—"

Christopher stood up and turned around to locate the troops.

"To the Hall of Rulers!" he yelled to them. They turned and ran through the crowd. Christopher ran to the table. The evil trees were approaching. He could see Crane and Four-Two making their way through the now disrupted crowd. Christopher pulled on Sir Two's leg as Sir Two argued with the crowd.

"But how are we to survive?" came the shouts. "What if we die out in the forest. What if it's true?"

"Is that what they've been telling you?" asked Sir Two. "Oh, haven't you been listening?" Christopher was up on the table now, pushing Sir Two with all his might. "You're a tree! Wake up, man, you're a tree! *This* is your city. *This* is your forest!" Christopher was now charging at Sir Two with his whole body, like one trying to break through a door. Finally, on the third charge, he unsteadied him and off the table they went. Four-Two and Crane approached as Christopher grabbed Sir Two's arm, pulling him, huddled and low, through the crowd. There was now a greater disturbance going on. They could hear Archer in the distance. Guards were coming from other directions. The crowd was murmuring loudly and moving outside of the lines that had been formed. Some were following Christopher and Sir Two to the Hall, only a few at first, then others. Soon they were joined by a mass of the crowd. When Christopher turned, he could see Four-Two fighting his way angrily toward him. Christopher pushed faster and reached the steps of the building. Looking up he saw the letters across: HALL OF RULERS. There, in the lobby waited the troops. Sir Two and Christopher ran in, racing for the gigantic winding staircase of marble along the wall. The ceiling of the Hall was high, and the staircase led to a second level that was a single corridor, resembling a balcony. Their troops followed, and the crowd poured into the hall.

"We can't go up there. Hey!" shouted one from the crowd.

For this was a meeting hall for the Rulers, and although it was a public building, no tree was allowed to the second level where the booths were unless they were fully prepared to enter one of those booths.

Many trees followed to the bottom of the staircase and looked up. Sir Two and six of his troops, whom he had selected beforehand, went farther up the stairs as the rest of the troops stayed behind. Christopher went with them, looking down at the crowd. They were high on the stairs, he could see the seven booths standing alone and majestic along the balcony floor. He stopped. Then Sir Two and his men stepped up and onto the floor.

"Okay, men, and Twenty-Four, you know what to do."

"Aaaarrghhh!" came a growl through the doorway. Four-Two had made his way through the crowd. He looked furious and frightful. The sight of him gave Christopher a start. Crane stood behind Four-Two, followed by some of the guards and more of the crowd.

Christopher looked back at Sir Two as each of the seven stood in front of the booths. For a moment Sir Two looked at him, and then he turned his head. The seven trees opened the booth doors and were gone.

"Boiling oil! Boiling oil is where you're going, squirrel!" It was Four-Two, making his way to the stairs. Christopher looked around him, then up to the booths. The crowd was restless, and he heard voices below.

"They've gone into the booths!"

"They're gone!"

Christopher scanned the whole room and every inch of the walls. There, on the wall along the staircase, halfway between himself and Four-Two, he saw hanging a shield with a coat of arms and two swords. Four-Two looked at Christopher suspiciously, his eyes darted, and they both raced to the swords, Christopher down the stairs and Four-Two charging up, pushing trees and what remained of the troops out of his way. He was a strong, large tree. When they finally reached the shield and stopped, Christopher stood face to face with the angry tree.

"Why don't you fight me first?" said Christopher, reaching his hand to the handle of the sword, trying not to show his fear.

"Why should I?" said Four-Two.

"What would they say about a tree who threw a human squirrel into a boiling pot without a fair fight?"

Four-Two thought for a moment, grumbling angrily and looking around. He reached a branch out to the other sword and again faced Christopher eye to eye.

They pulled the swords out and began to fight. The crowd became excited again. Christopher heard no sounds behind him. He couldn't turn to see if the seven trees had emerged onto the balcony.

"Where are your friends now, eh? I don't think they're coming back for you!" he said as he lashed at Christopher's foot.

William gasped and made a movement, but Christopher yelled, "No, William!"

The tree was strong and was overpowering Christopher as they continued up the stairs. As they neared the top, Four-Two pushed Christopher toward the railing. Christopher, sneaking out from under his grasp, found himself unexpectedly sitting on the railing and then sliding, face forward, down the winding staircase toward the crowd, his sword held high in the air. He could see William and the others below, watching him as Four-Two followed. The crowd cleared as he neared the floor with speed, jumping and turning quickly once he landed.

"Hah!" Four-Two was upon him again. "They're not coming back! Do you hear? You've led them to doom, squirrel!! And maybe we'll brand *you* instead!"

Christopher fought as well as he could. They moved out the door and into the courtyard. He was being overpowered as their swords clashed and swung. He could see William and some of the troops close behind.

"They're not coming back! Do you hear? They're gone! They're gone forever! And you'll be the one to blame! Forever and ev—"

And, suddenly, amid those angry shouts, those words more painful to Christopher than any sword piercing could be, just as fast as Four-Two was thrashing his sword, he was gone. The sword fell hard to the ground, clanking and cracking the marble. Four-Two had disappeared. Into thin air. Christopher stood, sword still in hand, out of breath, stunned. The crowd that had cleared around them fell silent. Christopher looked around and down at the sword. There was nothing but the crack on the ground, which ran to his foot. No sign of Four-Two anywhere. There was still a hush. Christopher looked through the crowd. He saw William standing close by, staring at him, his branches to his chin.

When they reached the hall, the rest of the troops began climbing the stairs, slowly, looking sadly up to the booths. The crowd looked up also, growing restless again. There were whisperings and shouts everywhere. There was no sign of Sir Two and the others.

Christopher wasn't sure what the troops were planning to do as he and William raced to the stairs. As they ran up, some turned to look down at them. When they were midway up the stairs, there was a sound. The crowd quieted again. They felt a slight rumbling beneath the building.

There were gasps and shouts, as they all reached for the walls and railing. Was it an earthquake? Had he sent Sir Two and his men to their doom? It couldn't be! The rumbling stopped. The trees all looked around.

"Look!" cried a tree.

Just then, one of the doors on the balcony had opened, then another, and then all of them began to open and out marched such a sight! It was Sir Two and the other six stepping out, all splendidly arrayed in bright, shining new uniforms.

These were no ordinary soldiers' uniforms: They were royal, red and gold, with medals and fringe and dazzling buttons. The trees were all smiling brightly. There were shouts and cheers from the crowd. The troops were jumping with joy and relief on the stairs. Some shouted, others shed tears and embraced.

~ ~ ~

After Sir Two's long speech telling of the new plans for Evergreen, Christopher knew that it was nearly time for him to go home. The whole crowd had tried to fit into the Hall to see the new Rulers since the word had already spread. But the gathering soon moved back out into the courtyard. There was celebration in the air, and the crowd was eager and ready to help, as though their eyes had been opened. The branding machine was destroyed right there on the spot, and those who had been branded received help in removing the marks from their bark. Christopher felt badly for those trees, for they seemed to be ashamed and it was a somewhat painful process. Cleanup and Rebuild crews were organized. Jobs were assigned or taken without conditions, only that the trees worked fairly, as had always been the case in Evergreen. There were plans to move the replanted Arboretum trees back from Tallaway, and no new trees were to be created in Arboretum.

One thing troubled Christopher: Archer, Crane, and some other trees were nowhere to be found. He searched for them in all the activity. He could only assume that they had retreated and would still be lurking in the forest.

Christopher wanted to visit the Polars one last time before leaving, and Sir Two took him there. There was much activity in the den as he stood among them. They seemed happy and restless. He was even allowed to pet them.

But he was still deeply troubled about Four-Two and the other trees. When he asked Sir Two about it, Sir Two just became quiet. He looked so regal in his new uniform.

"Come, Christopher," he said.

They were walking west to Tallaway. For a long time they walked in silence, Christopher and Sir Two, the sun shining around and upon them through the trees.

After a while Sir Two said, "You know Archer was originally from this area."

"Where?"

"This area."

"Here?"

Sir Two paused. Then, pointing, he said, "There."

Christopher looked in the direction Sir Two had pointed, to a cluster of trees in the distance. Sir Two was quiet. Christopher stopped.

Sir Two took a few more slow steps and then stopped. He did not turn around.

"Sir Two," Christopher began.

Sir Two was looking down at the ground.

"Sir Two where, exactly, was Archer from, I mean, do you know?"

Sir Two was quiet and motionless in the sunlight.

"Sir Two . . . "

Sir Two was still.

Christopher looked at the trees around him. He turned in a circle, looking around, just as he had done when he was lost, then looked back to where Sir Two had pointed. He walked closer to the cluster of trees. Closer he came to them, away from Sir Two, and then he stopped. Before him stood a tree, light and very tall. His eyes followed it up, way up, to where the glints of sun rested on its bark. Christopher stared at it for a moment and then took a step back. Something about this tree reminded him of one of the evil trees. His stomach sank . Christopher stepped back again. He watched as the sun shone peacefully upon it. He thought about the Mystery and felt saddened about the evil trees. He took another step, walking backward toward Sir Two and staring at the immovable trees. He turned and stopped, seeing Sir Two in the same position, his back toward Christopher, motionless. He hurried to the stilled form and reached for his branch under the felt uniform. Sir Two did not move.

Sir Two was as motionless as the other trees.

"Don't you want to—" Christopher began.

And then he saw Sir Two's eyes move. "No, I don't."

The rays of the sun continued to filter warmly down on them through the leaves as they walked on to Tallaway. Christopher loved the scent of the pine needles, and in their silence as they walked he realized he had been gone for three whole days.

"Can you really make me arrive back in time?"

"Surely, if the time frame is within reason."

When they reached Tallaway, Christopher said, "Will you tell William goodbye for me? I thought he was coming with us." Sir Two nodded.

"Now, let's see," Sir Two was taking out the pocket watch. "Saturday, eleven-thirty a.m., Field time. That should do it. Are you just about ready?"

Christopher nodded. When Sir Two took out the key, Christopher said, "I never did find my key, you know."

"Key?" asked Sir Two, turning.

"Yes, you know, the key I came here with, the one I used to get here. I dropped it in the leaves when you appeared."

Sir Two laughed.

"What's so funny?"

"Boy, you didn't get here on account of your key."

"I didn't?" Christopher was indignant.

"No," Sir Two said. "It's a good thing you lost it when you did, for it might have gotten you into trouble."

"Then how did I get here?" he asked, impatient now.

Sir Two paused between the trees and looked at Christopher. His eyes were teary from laughing. They were kind and familiar. He lifted his branch and for a moment touched the scar that ran down along Christopher's cheek. Then he smiled and said, "Boy, didn't I tell you that when you looked for me, I would find you?"

ABOUT THE AUTHOR

Wendy Cincotta is the author of the Evergreen Book series which chronicles the story of a boy and a tree come to life. Her play *Christopher and the Tree* has been produced at regional schools and its teleplay recently won as finalist in the Acclaim TV script competition. A Master of Arts graduate from Columbia University, Teachers College, she has done presentations at libraries, schools, bookstores and earth day events which incorporate artistic and environmental themes. She is a member of the National Writers Union, Playwrights' Platform of Boston and The Society of Children's Book Writers and Illustrators. Cincotta is also a classical and modern dancer and has performed in various venues in Boston, New York and the U.K.

Printed in the United States
40513LVS00002B/91-189

9 781589 614314